the

Daughters

of

Maine

by

Tish Thawer

Amber Leaf Publishing
Missouri

First Edition
First Printing, 2017
ISBN: 978-1543298512

Cover design by Regina Wamba of Mae I Design and Photography
Edited by Laura Bruzan

Amber Leaf Publishing, Missouri
www.amberleafpublishing.com
www.tishthawer.com

Praise for *The Witches of BlackBrook*

"Tish Thawer's intriguing story line is weaved and crafted into a magical and spellbinding web that kept me up until the wee hours of the morning biting my finger nails and cheering for the sisters. Strong story line and well developed characters that will sweep you away. I was completely floored by this amazing book and I recommend it to everyone.!" ~ *Voluptuous Book Diva*

"Tish Thawer is an amazing wordsmith. I have devoured several books by her and she never disappoints. The blend of history with contemporary is just genius and I can't wait to see what this author will come up with next. Add this to your list as a must read recommendation from me! An EASY 5 out of 5 stars!." ~ *NerdGirl Melanie*

"Overall, The Witches of BlackBrook was a grand slam for me. I was so enchanted by this spellbinding tale of hope, love, and a bond that can't be broken. There was something special about it and I honestly think it had something for all different types of readers. Whether you're into romance, historical, paranormal, new adult, etc. the author effortlessly weaves so many elements together to create a flawless experience for whoever picks it up. If you're looking to be enchanted and escape your mind for a couple hours, I highly suggest picking up The Witches of BlackBrook and diving on in!!" ~ *Candy of Prisoners of Print*

Praise for *Raven's Breath*

" ...this was an addicting, thrill ride of a read which kept me turning pages and cursing real life that kept interrupting me... A new take on a tale that is literally as old as time, I would challenge anyone to predict the ending. Brilliant!" ~ *NerdGirl*

"The plot is wonderful. The characters are amazing and fun. Tish Thawer's Raven's Breath is unique story. Meet the only female Grim Reaper...There are so many things that I love about this book but my favorite is the twist at the end." ~ *GoodReads Reviewer*

"...I now rate this story as one of my all-time faves. Raven is the first female Grim Reaper. One would think that would make for a dark, sinister story line. Well, it does, but not in the way you'd think. Ms. Thawer also breathes humor, light, and romance into this Sci-Fi novel. I love Raven's character, with her spunkiness, gumption, and self-deprecating humor. The scenes are lushly drawn, and the other characters grab your interest and add so much to an already wonderful story. If you've never read Sci-Fi before, read this as your first. If you love a great plot, read this. If you haven't finished it by Sunday evening, call in sick to work Monday morning. You'll be glad you did. I am so looking forward to reading the next in this series!" ~ *Amazon Reviewer*

Praise for *Scent of a White Rose*

"Thawer managed what I thought was an impossible feat. She was able to put yet another new spin on the age-old vampire tale." ~ *The Bookshelf Sophisticate*

"...everything about *Scent of a White Rose* was such a fresh new concept when it came to vampires, actually it was just a whole new concept in general for the paranormal genre! This is a read any paranormal lover should read!" ~ *YA-Aholic*

"*Scent of a White Rose* is not the plain Jane girl meets vampire and falls in love story...I will tell you that you should add this book to your TBR list." ~ *The Book Nympho*

"Tish Thawer crafts a seductive vampire tale with her eloquent writing style and keen sense of romance that simply entrances." ~ *Romancing the Darkside*

Also by Tish Thawer

The Witches of BlackBrook

The Witches of BlackBrook - Book 1
The Daughters of Maine - Book 2
The Sisters of Salem – Book 3
Lost in Time – (A Legends of Havenwood Falls novella,
and a Witches of BlackBrook side-story)

The Women of Purgatory

Raven's Breath - Book 1
Dark Abigail - Book 2
Holli's Hellfire – Book 3
The Women of Purgatory: The Complete Series bundle

The TS901 Chronicles

TS901:Anomaly – Book 1
TS901:Dominion – Book 2
TS901:Evolution – Book 3

Havenwood Falls Shared World

Lost in Time – (A Legends of Havenwood Falls novella,
and a Witches of BlackBrook side-story)
Sun & Moon Academy – Book 1: Fall Semester (A HWF
Anthology)
Sun & Moon Academy – Book 2: Spring Semester (A HWF
Anthology)

The Rose Trilogy

Scent of a White Rose - Book 1
Roses & Thorns - Book 1.5
Blood of a Red Rose - Book 2
Death of a Black Rose - Book 3
The Rose Trilogy – 10th Anniversary Edition

The Ovialell Series

Aradia Awakens - Book 1
Dark Seeds - Novella (Book 1.5)
Prophecy's Child - Companion
The Rise of Rae - Companion
Shay and the Box of Nye - Companion
Behind the Veil - Omnibus

Stand-Alones

Guiding Gaia
Handler
Moon Kissed
Dance With Me
Magical Journal & Planner

Anthologies

The Monster Ball: Year 3
Fairy Tale Confessions
Losing It: A Collection of V-Cards
Christmas Lites II

Acknowledgements

For all those who never stop looking for *more*.

"God and Goddess of the moon, stars, and sun, shine your bright blessing upon me as this new day has begun." — Tish Thawer

the

Daughters

of

Maine

Prologue

SALEM, MASSACHUSETTS

Present day

The cauldron bubbled and burped its putrid fumes into the small storage room Ann had called home for that last six months. Though recently cursed to live as a mortal, the magic she'd wielded for centuries still sizzled in her veins, reminding her of all the things she was no longer able to do.

The *tsk* of her tongue against her teeth marked the only reaction to the memory she'd allow herself, for the task at hand required all of her focus. Spells and witchcraft still existed, just not in the form to which she was accustomed. It took more effort and a multitude of ingredients when wielded by anything other than a *true* witch. Adding another pinch of fennel, she closed her eyes and began her spell. "Time is mine, fluid and true. Take me back, my curse to undo."

A pop crackled behind her, splitting the air and sparking the deep well of hope that still—even after all her failures—continued to live inside of her. "Yes! Come on. Open." Ann's eyes grew wide as the portal she'd struggled to create time and time again began to expand. Squinting, she peered through the sliver of altered space and found a crowd of cloaked witches milling about. She waited patiently to gauge the timeline, hoping this was where—or more importantly, *when*—she needed to be. The crowd grew quiet as four figures emerged from a cave.

"Welcome, my sisters and brothers. Our energy here tonight is what drew you to us, and now that our full powers are returned, we are to hide no more."

Ann scoffed as she watched Trin raise her arms into the air. *"Power heals and power binds, sending its call throughout time. Divided no more, united are we, the Witches of BlackBrook, forever the three."*

"Well, shit. I'm too late again." Ann flung a handful of black salt into the cauldron, snuffing out the power of her spell and systematically squashing the last bit of hope she had.

The brew sputtered and hissed, capturing her attention as a faint whisper floated to her ears.

"Do not quit, my child, your aim is true. Simply alter your destination and you'll emerge victorious."

A confident leer stretched across Ann's face as something far more sinister than hope began to swell from deep within her chest.

Chapter One

BLACKBROOK, NEW YORK
Present Day

Trin sat straight up in bed, shocked awake by yet another nightmare.

"Honey, what is it?" Jason asked, rubbing a comforting hand along her bare back.

"I'm not sure." She shook her head, her long auburn waves cascading side-to-side.

"This is the third bad dream you've had this week," Jason recounted.

Trin looked over her shoulder into the bright hazel eyes of the man she'd loved for centuries. Jeremiah, now Jason, remained her rock and understood all that had transpired while they'd been apart; from the very beginning when her spell separated her from her loved ones, to the demon and fellow witch that had kept them apart for all the long years, and the multiple lifetimes that had followed. Now here, reunited and transformed into their true selves, she held her teary gaze to his and bared her fears. "And just like the previous two, I can't remember a single thing about it. The feeling is always the same, though; something bad is about to happen."

Jason sat up, dipping his dark head to place a soft kiss upon her shoulder. "I think it's time to tell your sisters."

Trin shivered and shook her head, not ready for another earful from her newly reunited sister witches.

The smell of bacon permeated the air as Trin and Jason descended the stairs. Caris, aka Kara, her middle sister, was bent over the stove as she was every morning.

"Good morning, love birds," Caris called out. "How are you two on this beautiful day?"

"Morning," Jason and Trin jointly intoned as they each claimed a stool and slid up to the kitchen island.

Caris spun, sending her russet ponytail swinging as she cocked her hip and waved a spatula in their direction. "What's wrong?" she asked, piercing Trin with a concentrated stare.

"Nothing. I'm fine. Just another nightmare."

"What do you mean *another* one?" Kennedy sauntered into the kitchen fully dressed in a navy pantsuit, her dark-red hair tucked into a neat bun and her FBI badge securely fastened to her belt. "The last one you mentioned was weeks ago."

Trin lifted the glass of juice Jason had placed in front of her to her lips, using this moment to take in Kenna, her baby sister. Her confident, down-to-business aura was different from what she remembered in their youth, but there was no delaying the conversation that needed to happen today. "Yes. And when I mentioned it, you both brushed it off as nothing, so I didn't bother bringing it up again."

Caris's eyebrows shot toward the ceiling as she turned back to the stove to attend her bacon while Kennedy joined them at the island, her plate in hand. "Trin, it's not that we brushed it off as nothing, but ever since we stripped Ann of her powers and vanquished her to Salem, you've had all sort of *feelings* about the situation. Honestly," Kennedy lifted her fork to point at Caris's back, "we think it's probably just guilt."

Trin set her glass of juice back onto the granite countertop as gingerly as she could, considering her tightening grip. "Look, I know we've been apart for a *really* long time, and getting back into the swing of all things magical hasn't been easy for any of us, but I need you to remember that I'm your big sister, and if I say something's wrong, I would hope that regardless of our current station in today's world, you could at least give me the respect I deserve as your High Priestess and not make assumptions."

IPSWICH, MASSACHUSETTS
1690

"Kenna, Kara, please finish your chores so that we can make our deliveries and return before the moon fully rises." With a flick of her wrist, Karina sent two brooms soaring through the air towards her little sisters.

"Why do we have to clean every day? It's not like Mama is here to notice anymore." Kenna sobbed as she grabbed the broom and sank immediately to the threadbare couch.

Karina moved to sit next to her baby sister, knowing her words would only serve as a superficial tonic to the sorrow of losing their mother just a few months prior. "I know it's hard, little one, and I miss her too, but Mama left this house to me...to us," Karina gestured to both her sisters, "and like she said, if we take care of it, it will always take care of us."

Kenna wiped her dirt-soiled cheeks and nodded in understanding.

"Besides, the faster we're done and get these deliveries made, the faster we can get back here and continue our spell." Karina bopped Kenna on the nose.

The mention of doing magic together brought a spark to Kenna's eyes. Pushing off the sofa, her broom sang in a chorus of swooshes as she glided across the small living space at the front of their cozy little home. Kara had already finished in the kitchen and was moving to the back room where they kept all their supplies. "Do you think we'll need more herbs or candles to finish our spell?" she asked Karina.

"No. I've already gathered everything we need from the nearby field and creek." Karina dropped her head but couldn't hide her sad eyes. "With everything that's going on in town, we simply can't risk buying anything that would arouse suspicion."

Kara set her broom against the wall and pulled her big sister into a hug. "We'll be okay."

The rising tide of witch hunters and false accusations had already begun to spread through the land, and now with their mama gone, it fell to Karina to keep everyone safe. A responsibility she didn't take lightly. "I hope so, but I can't shake the feeling that something really bad is going to happen."

Kara pulled back. "Something worse than losing Mama?"

"Yes, I'm afraid so."

Chapter Two

The memory hit Trin hard. Knowing that the 'bad feeling' she'd felt was the catalyst to all that had followed during the burning times—including her own capture and persecution—certainly didn't help ease her mood towards her sisters' current opinions. "I understand that you may *think* I'm simply feeling guilty, but I assure you, it's more than that. We need to do a spell and scry for answers." Trin pushed off the kitchen stool and placed her breakfast dishes in the sink.

"Okay, sis. Let's plan to meet back here on Tuesday to work the spell. If this is as serious as you think, we'll need to use the full moon's power to clear our sight," Kennedy suggested. "Plus, I have to head back to Washington for a few days to finish up some work, so I'll be out of pocket until then."

"Why do you have to go back to Washington? I thought you used your magic to alter the minds of your employers so that you could stay away as long as you wanted," Caris asked.

"I did, but at the time it had only been us two," Kennedy waved a hand between herself and Caris, "so my magic wasn't as strong as it is now that we've found Karina and it's probably close to wearing off." She smiled at her big sister, hoping that despite their growing pains she knew how happy she was that they were all together again.

"Ah, I gotcha. Okay, well, Tuesday it is then. I'll check our supplies and make sure we have all the necessary ingredients," Caris confirmed.

Trin moved around the island so she could embrace them both at the same time. The loving energy that passed between them had become familiar again, and it never ceased to warm Trin's heart. "Thank you. And as far as Ann, yes, I do feel a tad bit guilty for banishing her, but only because I remember her as Kit and can recall all the good times we had together throughout the centuries. I do not, however, feel guilty that we stripped her of her powers."

Trin thought back to the time when Ann had been under the demon's influence and their nightmare had truly begun. Shivering, Trin turned to Jason. "I have today off and planned to spend some time with a few of our coven members, but since you're still on vacation too, I think I'd rather stay home and do some meditating with you, if you don't mind."

Jason's sexy smirk and wagging eyebrows sent her sisters into a fit of laughter, but Trin quickly explained, "Get your minds out of the gutter. I'm hoping to tap into some of Jeremiah's old memories of the other witches in the vicinity to see if there are any other threats we've perhaps overlooked."

"That sounds like a great idea," Caris agreed. "With Kennedy heading back to Washington, you'll have the house to yourselves for the entire day until I return from school."

"Okay, perfect," Trin replied. "We'll let you know if we uncover anything." She nodded toward Kennedy.

"Sounds good. I'll see you all on Tuesday." Kennedy waved goodbye and grabbed her briefcase, but stopped just before reaching the door. "Trin, please be careful. If you do find anything that worries you, promise me you'll wait until we're all together before attempting contact, okay?"

Trin sighed and leaned into Jason's comforting embrace. "Will do."

Trin busied herself by washing the dishes by hand and organizing the few supplies they kept in the kitchen for any impromptu casting they may need to do on the fly. She hadn't said a word since Kennedy left, and didn't plan to until Caris had vacated the house as well. Once the door shut, Jason approached cautiously and wrapped his arms around her waist before speaking over her shoulder. "I know it upsets you when they treat you like the fragile one of the bunch, but you have to understand, it's only because of how much they love you and that they're scared of losing you again."

Trin's shoulders raised and dropped in rhythm with her deep breath. "Yes, I understand, but what they don't seem to remember is that I am and always have been the strongest of the three." Trin spun in Jason's arms, bringing them face-to-face. "I'm the one who took care of them when Mama died. I'm the one who always kept them on task when they fought me at every turn. It's only because of me that they developed the powers they possess at all." Tears began to sting her eyes by the time she buried her head against Jason's broad chest.

"I know, honey, and again, I'm not defending their actions, but simply trying to explain. You were on your own for all those centuries, practicing your magic as much as you could with your bond hindered by Kit and the demon. But Kara, Kenna, and I were together the entire time, honing ourselves into the best witches we could be without you. It was tough on us not knowing how you'd react or how our energies would respond to one another once we were all reunited. I think that worry alone drove them to push themselves into becoming the witches you see today." Jason pulled back and looked Trin straight in the eyes. "They just wanted to be as strong as possible for you."

Trin maneuvered out of Jason's arms and walked into the living room, casting flames from her fingertips to light a fire within the hearth. "I know that too, but it's been hard for me as well. Thinking I'd been with Kenna all this time and remembering her as the petulant but sweet child I loved so dearly, only to find out that Kennedy is this hard-edged, kick-ass and take names kind of woman is something I never would've expected," Trin shook her head as she eased down onto the couch. "Don't get me wrong, it's not that I don't admire her for those traits and respect the powerful witch and woman she's become, but I guess my only problem is that, I just wish they'd give me the same level of respect instead of treating me like a ticking time-bomb ready to go off at any minute."

"I know, and I'm sorry babe. I think after spending centuries apart, we all thought coming back together was going to be easy, but here we all are, trying our damnedest to reacquaint ourselves with long lost versions of the past that simply no longer exist." Jason sat beside her and reached for her hand.

Trin stared at his strong, work-hardened hands and smiled. "You're right, of course. And perhaps what we need to do before scrying or meditating on some kind of impending doom, is perform a ritual just for us, welcoming our new-selves in a way that will not only bring us all closer together, but also honor the job the Goddess bestowed upon us."

"I think that's a great idea." Jason slid closer to Trin and placed a light but meaningful kiss upon her lips. "So, if we're not going to do any meditating today, how about we focus on my original idea instead?" He wiggled his brows again and felt Trin's mood lift immediately along with her desire.

"I like the sound of that."

Chapter Three

Caris flipped the key and shut off her Jeep after pulling into the school parking lot. Reaching for her cell phone she pressed the #2 key and waited for Kennedy to pick up. "Hey, are you okay? You seemed off this morning? Did Trin upset you?"

"No, not really." Kennedy sighed. "It just feels so odd having to tiptoe around the new emotions in the house. And you know me, I don't really do *strange feelings* and *gut reactions* very well," Kennedy replied.

"Yes, I do know you, and I understand those feelings are not only due to your training but also to the stringent rules you've placed upon yourself as our family's protector. You've become tough and hardened, which is a good thing, don't get me wrong, but you also need to remember it's not just the two of us anymore. Besides, you know as well as I do that we never had the kind of sight Karina did. I think we need to be more open and understanding of that too."

Dead air filled the Jeep as Caris waited for her little sister's response.

"I know you're right. And it's not like I'm making light of her nightmares, but there's more to consider now than before. We are all still getting used to the magic that has reemerged in us, and while I know that Trin has the best *sight*, I think she may need to focus a little more before deeming something 'bad' or 'evil', because you know as well as I do that emotions can alter your magic. It's like when you can control your pendulum just by thinking of the outcome you desire. I don't want her guilt about Ann manifesting into something that shouldn't have been a problem to begin with."

Caris knew why this was such a huge worry for her baby sister. She'd seen it too many times before during their past lives. One thing or another had happened that generated hope of finding Karina, or the opposite, some overwhelming fear that they'd not make it out of a particular lifetime alive. All the while, it was just false visions and misdirection being thrown at them by the demon they'd fought for centuries. "I get it, sis. I'll talk to her more tonight and see if we can all do some digging together. Maybe if Trin's able to bring us into one of her dreams, we can witness it for ourselves and get a better idea of what's really going on."

"Thanks, Car. You always have my back."

Caris smiled wide as the line went dead. "And you always have mine, little sister," she said to herself, tossing the phone into her purse. Her cheerful expression remained as she made her way into school. She liked the idea of dream-walking with Trin and thought perhaps she and Jason could obtain a little more insight before Tuesday when Kennedy returned.

"Good morning, Caris. Don't you look chipper today," greeted Principal Lyons.

"Hi, Sylvia. Thank you, I guess I am feeling extra positive this morning." Caris laughed.

"It's always nice to see someone excel at their job and with a smile on their face to boot." Sylvia waved herself off and proceeded down the hall, leaving Caris even more thrilled at receiving such a nice compliment from her boss.

After storing her things in the drawer of her desk, Caris finished sorting papers and was ready to greet her class for the day when her cell phone started to buzz.

"Hello?" Caris answered, not recognizing the number.

"Hello, Ms. Hardy. This is Dr. Weaver, I'm a professor at the University of Maine. As part of our ongoing family study, we have your sister's results in but haven't been able to reach her for the last few weeks. She has your number listed as a point of contact, so I was wondering if you knew how we could reach her, or if you'd be willing to offer your own blood sample so we could compare the anomalies we found during our research that I assume the two of you share."

"Um...excuse me? I think you may have the wrong person. I don't have any sisters currently in Maine. And my only sister has never participated in any kind of University study." Caris was careful to reference Kennedy as her only sister, seeing in this day and age, that was what the public records would show.

"Really? That's odd. This study is something we've conducted for years, and your sister has always participated in the interviews as well as the testing and genealogy study that recently opened up."

Caris rose from her chair and paced to the window, gazing outside at the beautiful fall leaves in an effort to calm her racing heart. "No, I'm sorry. My sister doesn't live in Maine, so like I said, I think you have the wrong person."

"I'm so sorry, but I have to insist on a few more questions, just to be sure before I can close this file."

"Okay, go ahead," Caris conceded.

"Are you Caris Hardy, a resident of BlackBrook, NY?"

"Yes."

"Are you a kindergarten teacher at the local private school there?"

"Yes." Caris took a deep breath.

"Clearly, I have the right phone number, so my last question is this, do you have a sister named Trin Hartwell?"

Caris swallowed hard. "Um. No, I do not." Caris struggled to mesh together a reasonable explanation, but she was too thrown to get a clear read on the situation. Trin had never mentioned being in Maine or participating in anything like this. But then again, maybe Kennedy was right and they really didn't know enough about each other in this lifetime yet. What if Trin had done something like this as a way to search for them before finding out the truth? Either way, Caris wasn't going to divulge any information to a complete stranger. "I'm sorry for your trouble, but clearly this is a mistake. I'd appreciate it if you'd remove my information from your records," Caris stated bluntly.

"Oh my, this is odd indeed, and I'm so sorry to have bothered you. Do you happen to know the woman claiming to be your sister?"

"No. I'm sorry, I don't." Again, Caris lied, knowing if they tracked her records through the regular means, they'd find her words to be true.

"Goodness gracious. I'm so sorry to have bothered you, Ms. Hardy. Please accept my apology."

"Of course. Thank you, and have a good day." Caris ended the call just as the morning bell rang.

"So much for feeling chipper," Caris snapped, tossing her phone back into her purse.

Chapter Four

"Hey, Trin, are you guys home?" Caris called out as soon as she stepped through the front door.

"Hi, Caris, yes, we're back here." Trin's voice rang out from the back porch.

Caris intended to approach this delicately, so she didn't make Trin feel like she was being attacked in any way, but as her frustration built throughout the day, it made it difficult to keep a level head. "Do we have any more wine?" she asked before even reaching the fridge.

"Yes, I think so. It should be chilled on the top shelf," Trin replied.

"Great!" Caris grabbed the sweet Moscato and poured herself a healthy glass, then joined Trin and Jason around the fire pit on the back porch.

"Bad day?" Jason asked, familiar with the tick in his cousin's jaw.

"You could say that." Caris sat in silence, drinking down half her glass before posing her first question.

"Trin, I received an odd call today and need to ask you some questions."

"Okay, sure. Shoot." Trin folded her legs underneath her on the chaise and smiled.

"Someone named Dr. Weaver from the University of Maine had my information on file as a point of contact for you. They said it was regarding an ongoing family study that you'd participated in and had given blood to. Does any of that sound familiar?"

Trin shook her head, confusion knitting her brow. "No. Not at all. I've never even been to Maine in this lifetime."

Whew, Caris thought. "That's what I figured, so I told her that I didn't know you, but it was weird. She had my name, occupation, phone number and said that 'Trin Hartwell' had listed me as her sister in the study."

"How strange." Trin uncrossed her legs and scooted closer to Jason. "Do you think it's something Kit, I mean Ann, could have done before we stopped her?"

"Oh, possibly. I didn't even think of that," Caris admitted. "She definitely would have had access to all that information, and maybe she was using this study as a way to track Kennedy and me without you knowing about it."

"Maybe, but why? That goes against her mission of keeping you guys apart, doesn't it?" Jason asked.

"Well, you know what they say...keep your friends close and your enemies closer." Caris lifted her glass into the air, satisfied they'd figured it out.

"Yeah, I guess that could be it," Jason conceded as he placed his arm around Trin's shoulders. "But why would she agree to giving blood to this study? Wouldn't that just prove that she wasn't related?"

"*Hmm*, I would definitely think so. The professor said that the genealogy part of the study had just opened up, though, so maybe that's why she stopped communicating with them; because she knew her jig was gonna be up soon." Caris shrugged.

"That, or because we ended her and the demon before she could return and get whatever results she was after," Jason added.

Trin sat silently, listening to their assumptions while trying to focus her mind on the internal warnings that had started to sound at the mention of Kit's blood.

"At least it's over, and I won't be getting any more calls

from them or have to worry about any strange blood trials regarding our family." Caris lifted her glass to her lips and swallowed the last gulp of wine just as Trin's eyes rolled back in her head.

"Oh my god! Trin, what's wrong?" Caris leapt to kneel at her sister's side.

Jason held Trin in his arms as she began convulsing against him. "Baby, please, what can I do?" he begged.

Caris bolted for the kitchen, returning in seconds with a clove of garlic and some ground valerian root. "Here, hold her while I put this in her mouth. It will help with the seizure."

Jason held Trin's head, caressing her cheek while Caris laid the herbs on her tongue. "Come on baby, come back to me," he whispered.

Trin's fit slowed immediately, but her eyes remained closed, squeezed tight like the knot in Jason's throat. He quickly pulled her into his arms and carried her back into the house. Caris, hot on their heels, followed them in from the back porch, tossing flames into the living room hearth then raced to the kitchen to mix up a batch of the healing tea Trin kept in full supply.

Propped up on the couch and covered with a cashmere blanket, Trin slowly stirred awake, coming to just as Caris handed her a cup of tea. "Thank you, I'm okay." She pushed herself upright, bringing the healing tonic gently to her lips.

"What happened? Are you sure you're all right?" Jason reached for Trin's legs, needing the feel of her under his hands to help calm his raging nerves.

"At the mention of Kit's blood, I got a bad feeling then a vision hit me swift and hard."

"A vision? What did you see?" Caris asked.

Trin swallowed another sip of her tea. "It was Ann for sure. I saw her surrounded by swirling tendrils of blood and two or three shadowy figures that I couldn't make out."

"Figures? Like more demons?" Caris spat.

"I don't think so. From what I could make out they looked like normal people," Trin explained.

"So did Heinrich at one point," Jason reminded them.

"I know, but there was something else odd about it; I couldn't get a read on the timeline. It seemed as though the other figures were possibly from the 1600s, but Ann looked like she does now, here, in modern times."

"That is strange." Caris collapsed onto the opposite couch, shaking her head.

"Do you think this has anything to do with the nightmares and bad vibes you've been experiencing?" Jason asked.

"I can't be sure, but I certainly hope not. Having to deal with anything about Ann or her past would be like opening Pandora's box. No good would come from it." Trin set her cup down and took Jason's hands. "But don't worry, whatever this is, we'll figure it out once we've completed our ritual." Trin looked at Caris and rushed to explain. "I was thinking we should perform a ritual between us three sisters to solidify our bond a little more before we start looking for trouble."

Caris nodded. "After this, I totally agree. We'll let Kennedy know once she returns on Tuesday."

"Sounds good." Trin smiled. "And thank you for the herbs and tea."

Caris jumped up from the couch then bent down and threw her arms around Trin's neck. "I'm just glad you're okay."

"Car, I'm fine. Don't worry. It takes more than a little vision to keep me down." Trin tried to sooth her sister's fears, instinctively knowing they stemmed from seeing their mama's attack first hand. Kara and Kenna had witnessed the moment that their mother had been spelled and fell sick through their scrying bowl, and Trin knew it was something that still stuck with her to this day.

Caris pulled back and wiped at her eyes, then stood and took Trin's cup to the kitchen.

"Are you sure you're all right?" Jason leaned close and whispered in her ear.

Trin ran her hands down his strong arms. "I promise, I'm fine. But I'll put some extra psychic protections in place before we go to bed, though, just in case. We'll definitely need to keep a close eye on things until Kennedy returns and we complete the ritual."

The phone rang, interrupting Trin as she laid out her plans.

"Hello," Caris answered. "What? You've got to be kidding me. Kennedy, this is bad. There's stuff that you should know first before you....DAMMIT!" She slammed the phone back into its cradle. Caris returned to the living room shaking her head and frantically ringing the dishtowel in her hand. "That was Kennedy, and you'll never guess where her next assignment is taking her."

"You're kidding me?" Jason's shoulder's dropped.

"Nope. She's been sent to investigate a case in Maine."

Chapter Five

Kennedy felt bad about cutting Caris off, but she couldn't risk a lengthy conversation with her boss staring her in the face.

"All set, Hardy?" Agent Nielson asked.

"Yep, let's go."

She'd finished submitting her paperwork from the *'BlackBrook assignment'* she'd used her magic to fabricate, but just as she'd began to weave a new spell to explain her upcoming absence, Nielson had walked in and demanded she join him. Knowing she didn't have to be back until Tuesday, she thought it might be prudent to actually do her job while she was here, especially if she'd like to continue receiving her government issued paychecks.

"So, what's the assignment?" Kennedy asked as she slid into the passenger seat of his sedan.

"Need to know, I'm afraid." His ornery smile, complimented by his sexy beard and piercing blue eyes, was the only thing that stopped her from probing his thoughts. She actually enjoyed his flirting...probably a little too much.

"Okay, but can you at least tell me where in Maine we're headed?"

"Orono." He winked.

"Ah." Kennedy nodded and settled in for the ride to the airport. She knew immediately they'd be taking the company plane, seeing that the state university was more than a ten-hour drive away.

The hour and thirty-minute flight was pleasant, but not as pleasant as Kennedy hoped. Nielson hadn't cast his gorgeous eyes in her direction for one second, but was instead preoccupied with phone calls the entire time.

"Anything I need to know before we begin?" she asked, hoping he'd give her at least a sliver of information as to why the FBI was headed into the University of Maine.

"Like I said, need to know. We'll be questioning some of the researchers who've reported an identity problem with one of their patients, and after that, we'll see where it goes."

Kennedy reached for her hip, securing her weapon, then pulled her suit jacket tight as they climbed the main stairs. "This is a case of identity theft, really? That's a little below our pay grade, isn't it?"

"Yes, well, since the identity involves your sister, I figured you'd want to be involved." Nielson's piercing stare and suddenly serious demeanor told her he was telling the truth.

Kennedy swallowed hard then quickly pulled herself together. "My sister? Caris?" she asked around the lump in her throat.

"Yes. And apparently someone named Trin."

What the hell? Kennedy cussed internally, wishing she could go back in time and finish her conversation with Caris. Obviously, they had more information than her as to what was going on here, and being left in the dark was one of her biggest pet peeves.

ISPWICH, MASSACHUSETTS
1690

"Why can't I go?" Kenna whined, furious about being left behind.

"Because little one, Beltane is for mature witches, not children," Kara explained a little too enthusiastically now that she was of age and able to attend this year's celebration.

"Enough." Karina walked into the kitchen dressed in her ritual dress and robe. "Kara, have you packed everything we'll need?" she asked.

"Yes, sister. It's all prepared. Thank you for letting me come to the celebration this year. It's my first official Beltane as a matured woman." Kara spun around. "Do you think I'll find my soul mate at the bonfire, or perhaps at the maypole dance?" Kara beamed.

"Perhaps, sister. Anything is possible when the God and Goddess join under the stars."

"Do you want to see the wreath I made for my hair? I can make you one too, if you'd like." Kara excitedly pulled the flower ring from her basket, displaying roses, daisies, and sprigs of baby's breath.

"It's lovely, Kara. But we need to be on our way, so gather your cloak and let's prepare to depart."

Karina turned to find Kenna staring up at her with a look of complete reverence. "You look beautiful," she whispered.

"Thank you, sweet girl. And I'm sorry it's not yet time for you to attend, but I need someone here to watch the house and take care of Pepper while we're gone." Karina reached down and ruffled the hair on their mutts head. "Can you do that for me, Kenna?"

"I guess so." Her lower lip overshadowed her chin as she walked into the sitting room and flopped down on the couch where she was joined seconds later by the bouncing hound.

"Good. Thank you. It will put my mind at ease to know our home is guarded by a powerful witch and her familiar. I'd also greatly appreciate it if you could refill my healing tea and keep the fire stoked beneath it while I'm gone." Karina leaned down and placed a kiss on Kenna's bowed head, silently sealing her protection spell in place.

Kenna watched her sisters leave then quickly bolted from the couch to lock the door behind them. "Come on, Pepper, let's check Karina's tea." The scruffy mutt followed her as she moved from cabinet to sink to hearth, making her tasks a little more bearable with each loving swipe of his tail. "I don't know about you, but I think something bad is happening. Karina is constantly brewing this tea as if she's aware of some impending doom that will soon be set upon us all." Kenna stirred the ingredients just as Karina had showed her, making sure they continued to steep just right. "But every time I ask her about it, she just tells me not to worry. It makes me so mad!" Kenna threw the spoon onto the floor, then quickly bent to retrieve it. Full of guilt, she walked to the sink and continued confessing to her pup. "I just don't think it's fair. Mama said we were all charged with keeping each other safe, and it's like they don't think I can do it. Like my magic isn't strong enough."

Kenna rinsed and dried off the spoon, then spun around and placed it on the table. "I'll show them." Pepper laid down in his usual corner once he felt her magic start to rise. A small whimper escaped him as Kenna spread out her hands, casting a thick layer of fog over the kitchen table. "Block me from their magic sight, let me be a witness this night. Charged to protect us sisters three, forever the watcher shall I be."

Kennedy remembered the exact moment her spell had sparked to life the bone-deep need to always protect her family. Then, after Karina was taken and everything went to hell in a hand basket, she was left traipsing from lifetime to lifetime, honing her mental and physical abilities to get the job done. Her sisters never knew she'd cast that spell and still didn't to this day, but the even bigger secret was how it actually hurt her soul when she couldn't do her job.

"You with me, Hardy?" Nielson asked with a raised eyebrow.

"Yeah. Sure. I'm good." With a slight shake of her head, she continued through the double doors, hoping she could pull this off without revealing her magic to her boss. She'd clearly need to dive in way deeper than just posing a few routine questions, and prayed to the Goddess that he'd remain none the wiser.

Kennedy followed Nielson down the stairs and through multiple doors into the research wing. They were waved through and ushered into the office of a Dr. Weaver, which was nothing more than a glass box within a larger glass box.

"Dr. Weaver, I presume?" Nielson asked the forty-something professor, her coiffed brown hair and white lab coat neatly in place.

"Yes. Hello. Please come in."

"Thank you. I'm Agent Nielson, and this is Agent...Kennedy." He opted for her first name instead of her last, then gave her a quick *just go with it* smile. "So what can you tell us?"

Kennedy took a seat in the corner, hoping she could just listen while letting Nielson take the lead. The lovely professor explained that their family study was one of the longest running, spanning almost sixty years, and boasted one of the largest research teams on the entire East Coast, and, of course, that they'd *never* had anything like this happen before.

"You said that the genealogy study had just opened up. Is that the first time you actually saw your participants face-to-face? When they came in to give blood," Nielson asked.

Kennedy smiled, knowing exactly where he was going with this.

"Yes. That's correct," Dr. Weaver confirmed.

"Do you happen to have any cameras in the lab that would have recorded the procedure?" Nielson stared straight at the camera in the corner of the office, but waited for the professor's response.

"Yes, of course. You'll have to excuse me for a few minutes, though, while I retrieve the footage from the security office." Dr. Weaver nodded, excused herself, then left the room.

"This should cut straight to the chase," Nielson boasted. "And once we get an image of this Trin person, hopefully you can quickly decipher how and why she'd have your sister listed as her own."

"Sounds like a plan." Kennedy remained seated, not wanting to disturb the spell she'd silently been creating. If Trin's blood was here for whatever research purpose or genealogy search she'd been using to find them, Kennedy was determined to get rid of it. They couldn't risk their blood being traced back through time, and honestly, she was pissed as hell that Trin had put them all at risk like this.

Nielson turned away and continued to scan the small office space while they waited for Dr. Weaver's return. Kennedy, on the other hand, took another deep breath and grounded herself down through the chair, past the layers of concrete, and firmly into the earth. To any onlooker, her eyes would remain open, because it was her third eye she closed to cast her spell. *"Through blood and bone, find what's mine, throughout time, the sacred line."* Kennedy's astral body floated from the chair and into the main lab, soaring directly towards the glass cabinets where all the blood was stored.

Magical lines of swirling energy were twisting and buzzing above one batch in particular, but no one vial was being precisely pinpointed. Kennedy strengthened her spell with a boost of power, hoping her boss didn't interrupt her concentration.

Again, snapping lines of energy raced back and forth, up and down, twisting and turning until they were nothing more than a jumbled mess.

"Here we are," Dr. Weaver's voice floated to Kennedy's ears.

Kennedy's astral body returned to her physical one just as Nielson inserted the disk and hit play on the computer. The footage was redundant, as patient after patient came in, stated their names for the camera, then filled out paperwork and sat to have their blood drawn.

"Is there any way to fast-forward to Trin's arrival?" Nielson asked.

"No, I'm sorry. The recordings are only by date, and this is the day we have on file for Trin's sample."

"Got it. Guess we'll just have to watch until she arrives, right?" Nielson asked.

"Yes, unfortunately. Would you like something to drink while you wait?" Dr. Weaver offered.

"No thank you, but don't let us keep you. If you have other things to attend to, please feel free. I'll text you once we're done."

Dr. Weaver nodded and left the two of them alone, having closed down the lab until their investigation was over. Nielson slid a chair in front of the desk and motioned for Kennedy to come closer and take a seat. "Okay, let me know when our girl shows up?" He patted her on the shoulder then dropped into her previously occupied seat against the wall, put on his sunglasses, and crossed his long legs out in front of him, clearly intending to take a nap.

Normally, Kennedy would razz the crap out of him for a stunt like that, but right now, the more privacy she had, the better.

She watched hour after hour of the clinical trial but had yet to see Trin on the screen. Nielson had stirred behind her a few times, but said nothing. Kennedy turned around, ready to wake his ass up and demand that he go get her something to eat, when suddenly a familiar voice sounded through the speaker. "Trin Hartwell."

Kennedy spun around and froze as she stared into Ann Putnam's eyes.

Chapter Six

Kennedy's magic flared as her protector side sparked to life. Within minutes she'd located *"Trin's"* case file, pinpointing the vial identification number which held Ann's blood. Casting a quick sleeping spell, she made sure Nielson wouldn't wake up as she took care of the situation. Once the blood was safely in her pocket, she destroyed all of Ann's records including her footage on the film. Lacing her work with a layer of magic, she assured none of the information would be missed. As a matter fact, it was now as if it had never existed at all.

Kennedy walked back to Nielson and placed her hands at his temples, molding the words she'd need him to say to Dr. Weaver to bring this case to a close. Seconds later, after lifting her sleeping spell, Nielson woke and texted the professor, alerting her that they were done and asking her to return to the lab.

"So, you're confident that this person isn't Trin Hartwell," Dr. Weaver asked.

"Yes, ma'am. We've identified the imposter and will be taking measures to secure her and correct your records once we have her official statement." Agent Nielson explained exactly as Kennedy had manipulated it in his mind. "Thank you again, we'll be in touch."

No, we won't, Kennedy thought. The moment they stepped outside the lab, Dr. Weaver's memory of this entire morning would be erased, leaving Kennedy to work the same magic on Nielson during their return flight.

"I still think it's odd that we were sent out here for a case of identity theft," Kennedy made small talk as they left the campus, needing a little more information before she'd feel comfortable bringing this to an end.

"Well, when you receive upwards of a million dollars to finish a sixty-year study that will impact the nation's health and wellness boards, not to mention taxes and insurance companies, you don't mess around with tampered records," Nielson summarized. "This study is government funded and therefore something like that gets noticed. Dr. Weaver notified us right away per their procedures." He shrugged.

Shit! Kennedy took a deep breath, hoping it hadn't gotten too noticed yet, or she'd have to dig even further to clean up this mess.

"Who else knows about the case?" she asked.

"Just you, me, and Dr. Weaver so far. She agreed to not notify the Board of Directors until we had answers. Once we get back, I'll put out a bolo on the imposter, get her statement, and book her for identify theft. After that, it's just a simple report to the University and all should be good."

Kennedy sighed in relief. *Yes, all would be good*—in about thirty minutes actually, once she erased the entire case from Nielson's mind.

"Okay, so do you want to tell me why I just saw Ann Putnam's mug on the security footage at the University of Maine?" Kennedy snapped into her phone.

Caris rolled her eyes and Trin shook her head as they both stared at Caris's cell that was blaring Kennedy's voice from the speaker.

"Well, like I tried to explain before you hung up on me, we think she went there and used all our information as a way to possibly track us down," Caris explained.

"Interesting, but why Maine? Why wouldn't she go to somewhere in New York when she was at one of her art shows as Kit. I don't get the connection," Kennedy admitted.

"We don't either but had planned to do a little more digging after you returned and we had a chance to do a ritual to help with our magic and sisterly bond." Trin cringed, preparing for Kennedy's response.

"Actually, I like that idea a lot, but how about we take this pony show on the road?" Kennedy quipped.

"What do you mean?" Caris asked, looking at Trin and shrugging her shoulders.

"I mean, why don't you two meet me in Maine, and we can take it from there. The Ann I saw in the footage was from the here and now, which means she could still be in the area."

Trin looked at Caris and raised a shoulder in agreement. "I'm okay with that," Trin answered. "I can clear my schedule for the rest of the week, which would give us six days including the weekend."

"Same here, I'll call in a sub for the rest of the week," Caris confirmed.

"Do you think Jason will be able to join us?" Kennedy asked.

"I doubt it. They're already short-staffed at the station, so I don't think he'd get approval for four more days off after just returning from vacation," Trin stated.

"Well, that's okay. If we need him to join us, he can always just come up on his next day off if we're still there," Kennedy replied. "I'll call and get us a hotel near the University and meet you there tomorrow night. You're closer than me, so I'll put the reservation in Caris's name so you guys can check in first."

"Okay, Kennedy. Sounds good. Is there anything you want us to grab for you?" Caris asked.

"Actually, I plan to take the 95 out of here and dip into Ipswich on my way up. It'll only add about an hour to my trip, but I think whatever ingredients we bring, getting them from our true home will only add to the potency of our spells, so I should probably be asking you that question; do either of you have something specific you want me to pickup?"

Trin's heart sank as she watched Caris's eyes fall to the floor. She knew they were both thinking about Lillian and her magic shop and how all the chaos that surrounded them had led to her death. Trin still carried the guilt of that and couldn't quite bring herself to ask the obvious question.

"Do you know who is running Lillian's shop now?" Caris asked, clearly the braver of the two.

"No, I was hoping you could tell me. You were always closer to her than I was," Kennedy's voice had dropped to a whisper, acknowledging just how hard it was for all of them to talk about this.

"I think it was passed to her daughter, Miranda. Just like us, they were always able to find one another in their continuing lifetimes."

Must have been nice, Trin thought to herself, still trying to get over the pain of being the demon's target all this time. Bound and misled by Ann time-and-time again was the only 'life' she'd known, and whether she wanted to admit it or not, it had left some pretty deep scars. "If you could grab me some nightshade, I'd appreciate it," Trin stated somberly.

"Um, okay. Are we trying to poison Ann, or just question her?" Kennedy asked.

"I guess I'll decide once we find out what she's up to." Trin walked away from the conversation and into the kitchen.

Caris sighed and quickly added her request, "I just need a couple more altar candles and some lavender oil. Other than that, I'm good. Just be careful and text me once you leave Ipswich. I love you, sis."

"Love you too, and please tell Trin I'm sorry if I upset her. I wasn't trying to," Kennedy whispered.

"I will, and I don't think it's you that she's upset with. We'll see you soon."

Caris pressed the end key and shoved the phone into her back pocket. "Hey, are you okay?" she asked Trin as she entered the kitchen.

"Yes. I'm just frustrated. I thought all this mess with Ann and Heinrich was over, but between my dreams and now this, I can't help but feel like we're still being yanked around like a bunch of puppets, and it pisses me off." Trin threw the wooden spoon she'd been stirring her tea with into the sink.

"Trust me, I know just how you feel." Caris hugged her sister then poured herself a cup of tea, sipping on the calming mint and lavender infusion. "I know you're upset that Jason can't join us, but I think it will be good for just us three to spend some time together away from here. Kinda like a mini-retreat." Caris smiled hesitantly, hoping to diffuse Trin's anger.

"You're right. We need to look at this as a way to get to the bottom of things while giving us a real chance to bond and solidify our magic." Trin nodded. "Thanks, Car. I guess we better get packing."

"I'm sorry you can't join us, babe, but Caris and Kennedy both agreed that we can do our bonding ritual first, which will hopefully help us find Ann quickly and put an end to whatever it is she's up to." Trin explained to Jason through the phone. "With our magic on point and our hearts aligned, we should be in and out and back home by the weekend."

"I get it, honey, but you're right, I hate that I'm not going with you." Jason sighed. "Just promise me you'll be careful and text me before and after you do anything when it comes to Ann."

"I promise."

"I love you, Karina. Call me when you get there."

"I love you too, and I will." Trin hung up and relished the warmth that had settled in her chest. Jeremiah had always had that affect on her, and she knew without a doubt, he always would.

Chapter Seven

IPSWICH, MASSACHUSETTS

1692

"Jeremiah, my love, I have to run to town to make my deliveries; is there anything that you need me to purchase while I'm there?"

"Karina, I thought we both agreed that we need to lie low with all that's been happening lately. I'm more than happy to continue accumulating our herbs from the woods, and there's nothing I need otherwise that I'd risk your safety for." Jeremiah reached for Karina's hand. "You're the only thing that matters to me. You and your sisters, of course. You are all my family now, even though you still refuse to make it official." He winked.

"My heart, body, and soul are already yours and will be until the day I die and even beyond. I don't need a ceremony or ring to know that." Karina leaned forward, placing a kiss on his lips and walked towards the door. "I'll be back soon, but if you want to use my scrying bowl to keep an eye on me, I won't mind."

"It's like you know my heart's intent even before I know it myself." He smiled shyly and waved goodbye, then retrieved the bowl even before the door had fully closed. Filling it half-full with water, he sprinkled the top with lavender snips and rose hips, then concentrated on the face of his beloved.

The vision of Karina appeared swift and clear, helping to put his mind at ease but also sparking his lust. He stared at her shapely figure longingly as she walked on the path that led from their home to the edge of town, carrying her basket of wares. Glancing around the room, he confirmed that Kara and Kenna were still out by the river gathering flowers and moss to dry, before working a little *magic* of his own.

"With sensual energy as your guide, stoke my desire as it flames to life. Pierce her heart and her core, reminding her of my love once more."

Jeremiah watched as Karina swooned, stopping in place and running a hand down the front of her dress. Spinning back towards the direction of the house, she smiled a sexy smile that confirmed she knew exactly what was causing her flush. He watched her lips move, then heard her sweet voice whispering on the wind. "I'll return soon my love, and then I'm all yours."

Trin woke from the memory as the Jeep bounced over a set of railroad tracks. She adjusted her jacket and smiled to herself as the reminder of her and Jeremiah's passion lingered in the warmth of her skin. "Do you want me to drive for a bit?" she offered, noticing they'd been on the road for at least three hours.

"No, I'm fine. I love a good road trip," Caris replied, taking a sip from her water bottle.

"Well, let me know if you change your mind. I'm more than happy to help out."

"Actually, I could use the help with something else." Caris cast Trin a sidelong glance, clearly feeling timid about her request.

"Sure, what is it?" Trin asked.

"With all this talk about genealogy and family studies, I was wondering if you could help me look up information on Lionel Epps," she asked, rubbing her reddening cheek with the back of her hand.

"Of course!" Trin took Caris's hand, remembering the spark between her sister and the junior Mr. Epps. The last Beltane celebration they'd all attended had been exactly what Karina envisioned it to be; the magical moment her little sister had met the man who could potentially be the love of her life. "I'd be happy to. I'm sure there's some records regarding the Castle Hill estate that could help. After that, if we need to do some spell work to locate him, I'm completely okay with that too." Trin squeezed her sister's hand, then dug out her phone from her purse to start her search with 'Siri's' help.

"Thanks, Trin. I know that Lillian said that some of the witches who'd been pulled through time didn't retain their memories of the past, but if there's any chance he remembers me, it would make me really happy." Caris shrugged like an embarrassed school girl.

"Well, you know as well as I do, that even if he doesn't remember you, there are ways we can make it happen," Trin wagged her eyebrows. "A little physical connection was all it took for me and Jeremiah, so maybe it will work the same for you and Lionel."

"Maybe. And wouldn't that be fun!" Caris laughed, enjoying their easy, light-hearted conversation.

"Okay, so I have to ask...did you and Lionel...you know, that night?" Trin bit her lower lip.

"Trin! Oh my goodness, I'm not talking about that." Caris blushed.

"What? We're all adults here, and it's not like we haven't lost our virginity time and time again throughout our various lifetimes." Trin shook her head. "I suppose it made it easier, knowing what to expect, but damn, I'm not going to lie, I'm happy to not have to do that again."

Caris and Trin's laughter filled the Jeep as they continued down the road towards their less than thrilling destination.

"Are you worried about what we're going to find?" Caris asked.

"You mean, Ann?"

"Well, yeah, but more so, what she's been up to."

"I'd be lying if I said no, and I definitely wish Jason was with us, but I'm glad that Kennedy is ready to take me seriously and treat this like the problem it could become," Trin stated.

"I can understand that, and I'm glad too. But like Kennedy, I'm curious as to what she's doing in Maine."

Trin shook her head and looked out the window, contemplating whether she really wanted to open this can of worms right now or not. *Oh well, here goes.* "Did you and Kennedy ever share a lifetime where you resided in Maine?" Trin asked.

"No. We didn't. Why did you?" Caris looked across the Jeep at Trin and gasped when she shook her head yes. "What?

How is that possible? I thought we always soul traveled to the same times?"

"I've been thinking about that a lot lately, and honestly, I'm not sure that's true. Every time I soul travelled to a new lifetime, it became easier and easier to find Kit. Like our bond was getting stronger with each hop. I think the opposite might have been happening to us, which over time weakened our connection and caused our souls to drift apart over time."

"Wow. I guess that would explain why we've been having the *issues* we have now that we're back together," Caris sighed.

"Perhaps." Trin agreed, still staring out the window.

"Do you want to talk about your time in Maine? Maybe it will shed some light on what Ann's up to," Caris suggested.

"I will, but I don't really feel like reliving it twice. Can we wait until we meet up with Kennedy and possibly get a good night's rest?" Trin asked, already committing herself to the upcoming conversation.

"Of course." Caris adjusted her hands on the wheel, not liking the sullen look on her big sister's face. Turning up the radio, she smiled at Trin, demonstrating her efforts to give her the space she needed.

SCARBOROUGH, MAINE
1703

"Mrs. Hunniwell, I'm sorry to have to inform you, ma'am, but your husband has been killed in a recent raid with the Abenaki." The British officer crossed his arm over his chest and bowed deeply. "My sincerest condolences." He handed her a sealed letter, then did an about-face and walked out the front door. Katherine Hunniwell had just lost her husband, and Karina Howe, had just woken up in a nightmare.

Karina stood still, rubbing the stiff piece of parchment under her thumb as information about her new lifetime filtered into her mind. She was in the middle of Queen Anne's War and her *husband*, Richard Hunniwell, had built this home for them in a field off Old Country Road after the small community was reoccupied in 1702. Richard had been a veteran of King Philip's War, and one of the signatories to Scarborough's incorporation in 1684. He'd been married before, but his wife and child had been killed in an Indian raid, which led to his implacable hatred of any and all Native Americans. This small community was abandoned in 1690 due to the violent raids, but after the English regained a small foothold, it was reoccupied once more.

Karina walked out the door and into the front yard, if you could call it that. Bleached stalks of tall grass surrounded the one-and-a-half-story Cape-style wood structure. It wasn't large, more the size of a small cottage, but Karina appreciated the clapboard siding and stone foundation, as it reminded her of her true home from which she was ripped all those years ago. Looking up to the roofline, she was happy to see sash windows and a four-light transom window sitting atop the main door. The house was sturdy and contemporary for the time.

She walked back inside and noticed the central-chimney, the small entry vestibule, and the winding staircase that led up to the attic. The decorations were minimal and suited Karina's taste just fine.

"Madame, are you unwell?"

Karina spun and came face-to-face with a pair of big brown doe-eyes. A woman with the most exotic caramel features she'd ever seen, including long black hair, braided and bejeweled with shimmering seeds and turquoise stones, was staring back at her from the middle of her very own living room. "Excuse me?" Karina mumbled, unable to think.

"Are you unwell? You look flush and confused, Madame Kate," the woman's rawhide dress shifted with her movements, setting alight the small bells and feathers sewn into its seams as she reached her hand out to Karina in a show of real concern.

"I'm fine." Karina clasped the letter to her chest, unsure of what was happening.

"It wasn't my intent, Madame, but I overheard the officer's message. I'm so very sorry for your loss," the Indian maiden offered in a soft display of polished English.

"Thank you..." Karina's words trailed off as the rest of the much needed information filled in the blanks within her mind.

Nadie was an educated Algonquin maiden who'd been helping her around the house whenever her husband, Richard, was away. He viciously abhorred Indians and would have punished her severely if he'd known she'd been welcoming the women of the tribe into their home as a way to build upon the peace that remained so very precarious in this region. Karina shook her head, *I guess that's no longer a problem I have to worry about,* she thought. She felt Katherine's grief over the loss of her husband and shared her sorrow. Katherine's life was still her own, but through the magic of soul travel, Karina was now a cognizant contributor to it all.

"Here, Madame, why don't you sit. I'll fetch you some tea," Nadie offered with an outstretched hand.

Karina nodded and slowly took a seat upon the nearest settee. She watched in awe as three other beautiful Native American women appeared from the other rooms and shuffled into the kitchen to help attend to her—their secret benefactor.

Chapter Eight

IPSWICH, MASSACHUSETTS

Present Day

"Miranda?" Kennedy inquired, addressing the thirty-something witch behind the counter of Lillian's shop.

"Yes, may I help you?"

Kennedy took in her kind blue eyes and long platinum hair and wondered if this was what Lillian looked like in her prime? The sisters had only known her in this lifetime, which was, for her, in the crone's cycle. "Hi. I'm Kennedy Hardy, Caris's sister."

"Oh my goodness, it's so nice to meet you. Mama talked about your family all the time." Miranda hurried around the counter and pulled Kennedy into a tight hug. "How are Trin and Caris?"

"They're good." Kennedy shrugged out of the embrace.

"Why do I get a feeling that's not exactly true?" Miranda's upturned smile and the spark in her eye made light of the fact that she'd just called Kennedy a liar.

Kennedy laughed. "Probably because your intuition is on point."

"Well, I won't pry, but what can I do to help?" Miranda gestured to the back of the store where they could talk in private.

"I need a few supplies and any information you can provide on Ann Putnam?"

"Ann Putnam? From our true time?" Miranda asked.

"Yes. We recently discovered that she was in cahoots with the demon your mother told Trin about, and was in BlackBrook with us until we stripped her of her powers and banished her to Salem," Kennedy explained.

"Wow. I'd heard the three of you had reunited and regained your powers, but that's some serious magic, right there." Miranda bobbed her head in appreciation.

"Yeah, well, it may have been all for nothing if we don't find out what she's been up to."

"What do you mean? What could she possibly be doing if she no longer has her powers?" Miranda handed Kennedy the bag of nightshade Trin had asked for, even before receiving their list.

"That's what we need to find out. We got word that she's been up in Maine and had used Caris and Trin's personal information as part of some kind of family study. We're not sure if she was simply using it to track us, or if there's more to it than that."

"Interesting. Weird, but interesting." Miranda handed Kennedy another bag of herbs, also on her shopping list they hadn't exchanged yet. "The only thing I remember about Ann is that she married some stranger no one had ever met."

Kennedy knew exactly who she was talking about. Heinrich had shape-shifted into another human guise at the time, probably to keep his little witch on the leash, no doubt. Moments like that had become clear to her and her sisters after they thwarted the demon and the link he had to Ann that day in the cave. Too bad they couldn't have gotten a read on those situations when they had originally happened, though; that would have saved them all a lot of time and heartache. "Hmmm. Okay. Well, thank you, and if you remember anything else, please give Caris a call." Kennedy smiled and accepted three candles, a bag of black salt, a vial of lavender oil, and a large chunk of celestite. "Looks like you got it all. How much do I owe you?" Kennedy asked, impressed she'd received everything she needed without ever showing Miranda the list.

"Nothing. You're good. Call this my contribution to help solve the problem." She smiled and returned to the front of the store just as the bell rang, signaling another customer's arrival.

Kennedy took a moment to look around the back room. She hadn't been here in ages, but nothing had changed in her absence. It still held fond memories of when Lillian would host her and Caris for tea, the three of them reminiscing about their true lives. Lillian talked about her daughter and her loving husband who'd passed just before Trin's spell, and how nice it was to speak openly about their magic after being forced to hide their true selves behind the borrowed lives they all lived for so very long.

Kennedy wiped an errant tear from her cheek and gave thanks to Lillian, knowing her prayer would be carried to her ears on the back of the Goddess's wing.

"Hey, I'm sorry, but I think I remember something else about Ann," Miranda whispered, interrupting Kennedy's reverent reflection.

"Oh, okay. Great, what is it?" Kennedy quickly composed herself.

"I think she had nine sisters."

"What?"

ORONO, MAINE

Present Day

"Nine sisters? You're sure?" Trin asked as Kennedy dumped their supplies onto the hotel bed.

"Yep, that's what Miranda said."

"I don't remember anything about the Putnams, so I'm lost here," Caris admitted.

"It seems like we're all lost here," Trin flopped into the high-back chair, discouraged and tired.

"Well, at least it's something to go on and possibly an explanation as to why she was trying to participate in a *family* study. Maybe she wasn't looking for us, but trying to find her true sisters instead," Kennedy suggested.

"It makes sense, for sure, but why would she pretend to be Trin then? Why wouldn't she just state who she really was?" Caris asked.

"You mean say that she was Kit? A person who had no family ties in this century at all?" Trin asked.

"Well, yeah, I just don't get why she'd involve you or me if she was really trying to find her own true family. It just doesn't add up." Caris shrugged.

Kennedy tossed her badge onto the nightstand. "None of this adds up. Ann shouldn't even be a threat at all right now. If you ask me, she deserved way more than she got. We were too light on her. Clearly." She glared at Trin. "We stripped her of her powers and honestly, regardless of why the hell she wanted to do a genealogy search, I just don't see what kind of trouble she could really cause if our spell did its job," Kennedy snapped, frustrated at the whole situation.

"Well, I guess that's what we're here to figure out," Caris smiled, trying to diffuse the tension in the room. "Now, how about we order some room service and tackle all this first thing in the morning?"

Trin nodded, appreciative of Caris's attempt to calm their sister down. "Sounds good to me."

"Same. And hopefully by tomorrow night, we can all head home, stress-free and ready to lead the coven in the upcoming Imbolc celebration," Kennedy smiled and eased down onto the opposite bed, clearly trying to make peace as well.

"If you'll excuse me, I'm going to step out and call Jason real quick while we wait for the food. If you could just order me the cobb salad, that would be great, thanks." Trin waved her cell in the air then stepped out into the hallway, turning to walk back to the atrium she saw on their way in.

"Hi, babe. Everything okay?" Jason asked.

"I don't know. Tensions are running high, and it's almost like Kennedy blames me that we're even here." Trin sighed.

"Oh, honey, I'm sure that's not true."

"She said that if our spell to strip Ann of her powers had worked like it should, then she shouldn't be a threat despite whatever it is she's up to." Trin shrugged although no one was there to see it. "That one stung a bit."

"Yeah, that was definitely out of line. And besides, we all know for a fact that the spell worked, so I'm not sure why Kennedy would say something like that." Trin could hear the rising anger in Jason's voice.

"I'm sure she's just frustrated, but still, I'll be happy when we get to the bottom of all this," Trin confessed.

"Me too. I want you home. I miss you."

"I miss you too. How was work?"

"Same old, same old. Nothing interesting to report in the mundane world of BlackBrook." Trin could sense his smile through the phone.

"Well, that's one good thing then. Get some rest, and I'll call you in the morning. I love you, Jason."

"I love you too."

Trin pressed the end key and took a moment to look out over the wall in garden. The lush ferns and hostas mixed beautifully with the lily-of-the-valley and snowdrops that wound through the dark mulched pathway stories below.

"Beautiful isn't it?" a husky voice asked from over Trin's shoulder.

"Yes, it definitely is." Trin turned and smiled, then quickly moved back down the hallway.

"Before you go, can I ask a favor?" the stranger asked.

Trin looked back but didn't respond.

"Tell Kennedy her boss would like to talk to her."

Chapter Nine

Trin gasped as she rounded the corner, smacking straight into Kennedy and Caris.

"What's wrong? We felt your energy spike," Caris asked, grabbing her by the arm.

Trin flipped a thumb over her shoulder. "Kennedy, your boss is here and said he wants to talk to you."

"What?" Kennedy leaned around the corner but saw no one. "Nielson's here?"

"Yes. He snuck up behind me and then said to tell you he wanted to talk. It was kind of creepy."

Kennedy took a step in the direction of the elevator, clearly intent on confronting her boss right away but stopped short when Trin pulled on her arm, yanking them all back to their room.

"I thought you cast a memory spell on him, so why would he be here?" Trin flipped the lock and started picking at her food, hoping to settle her nervous stomach.

"I did! That's why this is so odd. I erased his memory of the case at the University, and then cast the necessary spell to justify my extended absence." She slammed her fist against the door. "Dammit! Why is this happening?"

"Maybe something is wrong with our magic," Caris said around a bite of her crab cake.

Kennedy forced herself to take a couple of deep breaths. "I don't like the sound of that, but maybe Caris is right. A thread seems to be unraveling here, and the outcome doesn't seem to be in our favor. We need to do our ritual and we need to do it now," Kennedy stated.

Trin nodded. "Let's finish our dinner so our energy is at its peak, then we'll get started."

Hesitantly, Kennedy and Caris joined her around the table, casting Trin's thoughts back to another time.

IPSWICH, MASSACHUSETTS
1692

"Kara, place the bread on the saucer, and Kenna, pour the wine into the chalice," Karina instructed.

"What spell are we doing tonight," Kenna asked, always ready to hone her magic.

"Tonight we're going to use the full moon's energy to call forth our personal power, boost our protections, and increase fertility." Karina blushed.

"Someone feeling ripe?" Kara teased.

"Hush, now. It's not just for me and Jeremiah, but for the livestock and crops as well." Karina glided around the table, setting the tools and candles in their place.

"Well, I'd be really happy if we could welcome a baby into the family," Kenna beamed.

"Me too," Kara added.

"We'll see about that, but first...magic!" Karina held her hands over the table and smiled when the flames burst to life. "Goddess bright, on this night, join us now and hear our vow. Together we thank you for all you do, in and out of the circle true. We humbly ask that our needs be met, no more no less than you see fit." Karina nodded at Kara and spoke into her mind, *"Lift the bay leaves one at a time and read what's scribed upon them."*

Lifting the first leaf, Kara intoned, "May our personal power grow this night, strengthening our love and might." She glanced up expectantly at her big sister.

"Good. Now set it to flame and toss it into the cauldron." Karina mentally instructed.

Kara held the leaf over the candle nearest her, then tossed it into the waiting vessel.

"Kenna, you next."

"May all we love, protected be, boosted by our powers three." Kenna lit her leaf then tossed it in, just as her sister had.

Karina lifted the last leaf and placed a kiss upon it. "Grow our bounty in numbers and strength, continue our line to the edge of times brink. Sustained and cared for, all are we, by the Goddess's grace, so mote it be."

"So mote it be," sang the girls in unison.

"Where do you want me to spread the black salt?" Kennedy asked, pulling Trin from yet another trip down memory lane.

"Let's move the table and chairs and do it here. This should be sufficient," Trin instructed, clearing their plates and drinks, while Caris and Kennedy moved the hotel room furniture out of the way. Placing the small altar cloth she'd brought from home in the center of the floor, Trin placed the celestite crystal and the three candles in the middle of it and then took a seat as Caris joined her, signaling Kennedy to cast their circle.

"I cast this circle once around, all within by magic bound; protected by the Goddess are we, strengthened by earth, so mote it be." Kennedy sprinkled the black salt around them in a circle.

"So mote it be," Trin and Caris repeated.

Kennedy joined them cross-legged on the floor and watched as Trin raised her arms and lifted her eyes to the ceiling.

"My Lord and Lady, we ask that you join us this night for our sacred rite. To reconfirm our bond as sisters so true, for power and love is achieved only through you." Trin closed her eyes as her words brought the Goddess's power to life within her. A pulse of pure white energy burst from the crystal, lighting the candles and knocking the girls backwards as it spread outward toward the edge of their circle. All three siblings pulsed with divine energy, and together fell into their astral states. *"We are here to follow your lead, guide us Great Goddess, to reclaim our magical seed."* Trin's words floated through the ether as the three sisters soared toward the heart of the Goddess's domain.

Stilling at the sight of a large cherry tree, Trin noticed her mother's pendant hanging from a low branch, and beside it, swinging in the breeze, was the ring Jeremiah had given Karina all those centuries ago, the same one Jason now wore around his neck. Both talismans spun, catching the reflective light of the full-moon as the Goddess's words flowed into their minds. *"Here at the cherry tree, both feminine and masculine, this sacred wood is connected to the heart of the Earth. Use its grounding energy to find your center again; solid and unwavering and imbued with the love and power of those not present, its magic will stabilize and focus your intuitive sight and lead you to the path where obstacles melt away. Allow its healing and love magic to flow through you, for the cherry tree is a source of detection and unification. So mote it be."*

"So mote it be," they replied in unison.

The Goddess's words felt more like a reprimand than a spell; humbled and enlightened, they all floated toward the tree, each placing a hand upon its thick trunk. White hot energy shot into their palms and straight to their hearts, providing each their own private vision.

Trin was flooded with memories of their mother, Jeremiah and her sisters, as well as Kit and all the other incarnations of Ann throughout her multiple lifetimes. Anger, guilt, remorse, and love twisted her stomach into knots as she was forced to open herself and face the truest feelings buried deep inside her. She'd loved Kit, and every other person Ann had been, and felt the guilt of that all the way to her marrow.

Caris's mind was full of lost love and mediocre lives lived. Nothing special and nothing gained from each new phase of their soul travel. She was weary and tired, and wasn't sure exactly what she had to offer to the group. She felt herself shrinking as feelings of inadequacy crippled her.

Kennedy's heart was full of fear, anger, and regret. Images of her terrified, always crouching and fearful of losing the ones she loved spun around her like a tornado. Unable to fulfill her role as protector and angry that she was never taken seriously by her older sisters. She had changed the most out of her siblings, and it became clear that that change had a lot to do with the wedge between them now.

Suddenly the three sisters' astral bodies floated together in the center of a vortex, swirling just below their feet. Each of their previous visions were now on full display behind them, like movies being projected onto a large, foggy screen. The Goddess's voice boomed into their minds, *"Release your fears and the woes of your heart, and know that after leaving, nothing will tear you apart. Forgive and forget and to yourselves be true, for there is no blame being put upon you."* The girls' visions spun and melted, swirling down the spiral vortex and along with it, their sorrowful memories. *"Go now, my powerful daughters, and find the source of the true issue at hand."*

Opening their eyes, Trin, Caris, and Kennedy woke back in their hotel room with a deep sense of love and focused purpose. Sitting up, Trin concluded their ritual. "Thank you, my lady, for joining us this night. May we strive to honor you and fulfill your wishes now and always. Merry did we meet, merry may we part, and merry shall we meet again." They linked hands and sat in silence as the magical energy in the air began to dissipate, leaving them energized and at peace with themselves and each other.

"I want to say I'm sorry, but know if you're both feeling like I am, it's not necessary, but still; it would make me feel better to say it," Kennedy squeezed her sisters' hands.

"I feel the same way," Trin smiled kindly.

"Well, now that we've been whipped back into shape, how about we get some rest and start tomorrow off with a scrying spell to locate Ann and really get down to business?" Caris insisted.

"Sounds good, but first things first; my initial spell of the morning will be to locate my boss and find out what the hell is going on," Kennedy fumed.

Chapter Ten

Jason woke to an empty house for the third day in a row. "This sucks," he confessed out loud. Padding down the stairs, the silence settled in his bones and left him as uneasy as one of Trin's dreams. The coffee pot sputtered, having been programmed the night before, bringing him to his first stop in his journey towards calm. "*Mmmhhh.* The best part of wakin' up..." he let his off-tune jingle die out as he brought the cup to his lips. "Ah! That's better." He lived in a house full of women who loved tea, and not that he didn't, but having a pot of coffee on twenty-four-seven had been about the only highlight of this forced separation.

Reaching for his phone, he dialed Trin and got her voicemail. *"Hello, so sorry I missed you. Please leave a message after the beep and I'll get back to you as soon as I can."* Jason sighed and waited for the beep. "Babe, it's me. Call me back when you can. I want to know what's going on and have to leave for work soon. Okay. Bye. Love you." Bounding back up the stairs, he debated opening his third eye and peering into the situation first hand, but after the last talk they'd had, he wondered if Kennedy should be the one he took a peek at instead of Trin.

Just as he settled into the chair on the balcony, his phone buzzed in his hand. "Babe, hey. How's it going? Everything okay?" he asked Trin.

"Yes. We're fine. Better than fine, actually. We're getting ready to do a couple scrying spells,"

"A couple?" Jason interrupted.

"Yeah. Kennedy's boss showed up out of the blue, and she's feeling a little uneasy about it, then after that's handled, we're going to start searching for Ann."

"Okay, well, please be careful. I'm headed into work here in a few, so I'll be out of reach for most of the day. If you need me though, you know how to find me." He closed his eyes and sent a surge of his affection through the ether.

"Indeed I do, and I love you too," Trin whispered.

Jason hung up the phone, feeling relieved yet anxious at the same time. "Damn this shift rotation," he cussed, wishing more than anything he could be with the ones he loved.

ISPWICH, MASSACHUSETTS
1693

Jeremiah felt Karina's fear spike and then her overwhelming anger. He knew he wouldn't reach her in time and he was right; by the time he'd arrived at the Howe's cabin, Kara and Kenna were crying into each other's arms and relayed the message that Karina had mentally sent to them both. *"Do nothing. I will take care of this."*

He attempted to reach her mind, but found she'd put up a block, probably in fear of other true witches in the prison trying to penetrate her mind. He couldn't stand by and do nothing, though, not when it was his Karina.

Jeremiah raced around the kitchen and the store room, gathering his needed supplies. Muddling the ingredients, he swallowed them in one gulp and cast his spell. "Space and time, bend to my will, transport me now, to my love I appeal. Take me there, body and soul. To save my love, the only goal." The air shimmered and bent in on itself, and with a *pop*, he was gone.

Reformed, Jeremiah looked up to find his beloved Karina lying on the cold stone floor of the prison. He reached for the door, sending a jolt of magic to disable the lock then entered her cell.

"Why did you come?" she asked.

"How could I not? I love you, Karina. So be it if I get caught using my magic to reach you. If you're going to burn, I'll burn with you." Jeremiah enveloped her in his arms, holding her close as she sobbed into his chest. "We'll figure a way out of this, I promise," he swore. He could feel her slipping away.

"No, we won't. Nothing I do will keep me from the stake. I've accepted it and so should you."

"I can't let them hurt you." Jeremiah kissed her hair, pulling her tight, already knowing she was going to force him to let her go.

"You don't have a choice. But what I do need is your promise. Swear to me that you'll always look after my sisters. Protect them when I'm gone," Karina pleaded.

Everything in him hurt. "I swear it."

Karina placed a soft kiss upon his lips and pulled herself together. "They'll be here soon, you must go."

Heartbroken but resolute, Jeremiah kissed his beloved again, then looked back one last time as he shut the metal door and disappeared.

Jason wiped the tears from his eyes. Remembering the most painful, heartwrenching moment of his life was never easy. He'd recalled that particular memory so many times over the centuries, searching for something he could have done differently.

"Screw this!" He slammed his hands down on the bathroom counter and pulled out his phone. "Captain Morris, please. It's Hardy. Thanks." Jason paced across the tile, hoping he wasn't making a mistake. "Captain, good morning. I'm sorry to ask, but I've had a family emergency and need to request a few more days off. Yes, I understand. Okay, thank you, sir. I'll put in for the next rotation as soon as I return. Thanks again."

Hanging up, Jason smiled wide and rushed to the closet to grab his suitcase. "I'm coming baby, and this time, there's nothing you can do to stop me from helping."

"Are you sure you want to do it this way?" Caris asked Kennedy.

"Yes. I know it's easy to use our magic, but honestly, I think the quickest way to find out if he's here is just to ask." Kennedy shrugged as she picked up the hotel phone's receiver.

"Hi, yes. This is Ms. Hardy in room 618, do you have any messages for me? No, okay, then could you please tell me what room Mr. Nielson is in? We are supposed to be having a meeting this morning. 412. Got it, thank you."

"Wow. That's impressive and a little scary. I didn't think they were supposed to give out that kind of information," Trin asked.

"I didn't say I wasn't going to use magic at all," Kennedy smirked, tapping her right temple.

Trin laughed. "Ah."

"So, as you heard, he's here and in room 412. Guess I'll go pay him a visit and see what's going on."

"Do you want backup?" Caris asked.

"No. I'll be fine. If I have to erase his memory again, I'll just do that. Now that our powers are inline, it should be fine."

"Okay, but if anything is off send us a warning, and we'll come running," Trin nodded, suddenly serious.

"Will do, sis." Kennedy hugged her big sister for the first time in a long time and headed out the door. Walking to the elevator, she pushed the down button and waited.

"I wondered how long it would take you to come looking for me," Nielson said from over her shoulder.

Kennedy turned around, slow and confident. "Not long, since you basically accosted my sister all cloak-and-dagger-like. What was up with that? Why didn't you just call me?" She positioned herself with her back towards the open end of the hallway.

"I wanted to be face-to-face when I asked why you lied to me?" Nielson cocked a brow but remained in place, leaning against the wall with his thick arms crossed over his chest.

"What are you talking about?" Kennedy asked, wondering which lie he was referring to.

"I'm talking about the fact that you do know a Trin Hartwell. She's living in your home for Christ's sake."

Kennedy's eyes grew wide. Her magic had never slipped before, and it left her tongue tied.

"Why did you act like you didn't know her this entire time? Why lie to me?" Kennedy could feel Nielson's anger, but it was more than that. He was hurt.

"I didn't think it was pertinent to the case. Trin, the *real* Trin, wasn't the issue here, it was the person who was pretending to be her...*that* was our focus." Kennedy shrugged. "My family's personal life shouldn't have had anything to do with it."

Nielson rubbed his chin as Kennedy began to mold his thoughts to accept her excuse at face value.

"I suppose you're right, but at the same time, it feels like you were hiding information that could have been important."

Kennedy concentrated harder.

"I wasn't hiding anything from you, as a matter of fact," she walked forward—needing to seal her spell with a physical touch, "you need to just forget this case and return to Washington. Your expenses here were for nothing more than personal leave." Kennedy smiled and released Neilson's arm as his eyes began to dull and his body relax. "Now go back to your room and get some rest, then book the first flight back to DC tomorrow morning." Kennedy blew a magic-laced breath into his face, then turned and walked away, happy to know her relationship with her boss was still safe after all.

"So what happened?" Caris asked the second Kennedy walked back into their room.

"You were right, our magic must have been diminished somehow, and he remembered something about the case he shouldn't have. It's okay, though. We're good now. I recast the memory spell, and he'll be on his way back to Washington tomorrow morning none the wiser." Kennedy grabbed the map from the desk and spread it across the mattress. "Now, let's find Ann. Are you ready, Trin?"

"Wait a minute. Are you sure you're okay?" Caris interrupted. "I know you care for him," she stated flatly.

"Yes. I do care for him, he's a really good guy. I hate having to use my magic to manipulate him, but we all know it's for the best." Kennedy shrugged. "So, come on, let's get focused and deal with the problem at hand so we can all get back to our lives." She ground her lips into a tight line as to not betray her desire to share that life with Nielson in a much more personal way than their current superior/employee relationship.

Trin smiled and pulled a delicate fluorite pendulum from a black satin bag and nodded to Caris. "Join me with yours."

Caris moved towards the edge of her bed, pulling her rose quartz pendulum from her pocket. "All set."

"What do you want me to do?" Kennedy asked, not really one to use the pendulum that often.

"Just stand near us to lend your energy and repeat any chant that I start," Trin smiled.

"Gotcha!" Kennedy moved into position next to Caris.

Holding her pendulum out, Trin waited for Caris to do the same then began the spell. "Find the one we're looking for, Ann from now and before. Reveal to us what hides within, my Lord and Lady, let the search begin."

Both pendulums spun in a circle, faster and faster until they flew from their respective owner's hand, landing with their points touching over one particular spot on the map.

"Wow. That was quick," Kennedy stated.

"Do we recognize this place?" Caris asked, hoping she wasn't the only one at a loss.

Trin sighed. "I do. Remember when I said I'd spent a lifetime in Maine..." her words trailed off.

"Yes," Caris replied as Kennedy shook her head no.

"Well, Scarborough is where I lived. It was 1702."

"Where the hell were we?" Kennedy asked, looking at Caris.

"I have no idea."

Chapter Eleven

Repacked and back on the road, Kennedy followed Caris and Trin down the I-95 towards Scarborough. Trin had given them the rundown of the lifetime she'd spent there, which was still so hard to believe, not to mention completely disconcerting since she and Caris had no idea where they'd been during that time period. Trin was hopeful that once they were back on *familiar-to-her* soil, they'd be able to find Ann and get some answers. *I sure hope so*, Kennedy thought, fighting against the uneasy feeling creeping up her spine.

In the Jeep, Trin's phone buzzed and displayed Jason's face on her screen. "Good morning, handsome, how are you? I miss you." Trin smiled as she spoke.

"Hi. Well, I was great until I realized my surprise was a bust. Where are you? I came to Orono to meet up with you guys." Jason's voice was warm but edged with annoyance.

"Oh, honey, I'm so sorry. We got a lead and are headed down to Scarborough as we speak." Trin looked at Caris and cringed, feeling bad their change in plans had affected his efforts to come join them.

"Okay. Let me grab a bite to eat then I'll fill up and be on my way. I'll meet you there. And oh yeah...Surprise!" He coughed out a laugh.

"Oh, babe. Thanks for coming. We'll see you soon. I sure love ya." Trin smiled into the phone.

"Love you more."

"I knew he wouldn't be able to stay away," Caris teased.

"Do you think it will bother Kennedy that's he's joining us?" Trin asked.

"No. Not at all. Jeremiah's always been there for us."

IPSWICH, MASSACHUSETTS
1693

"What do you mean she's chosen to burn? NO! We have to get

her out of there. I can't lose her too," Kenna sobbed.

"I'm sorry, there was nothing I could do that would change her mind. She has something planned, I'm sure of it, but all we can do now is wait and trust her," Jeremiah pulled both sisters into his arms. "Karina's charged me with your care, and you need to know, I'll never leave you."

They spent the night crying and grieving the loss of their beloved Karina. Frightened and scared of what the future would hold, they each created a talisman that would keep Karina's spirit close to their hearts. Jeremiah fashioned a length of leather cord to hold the ring he'd purchased for her in hopes of making her his wife. Kara gathered the herbs her sister used for her healing tea and placed them inside a poison ring she wore on special occasions. Kenna reached into Karina's special drawer of their workspace and pulled out her Book of Shadows. Pulling the spell which she used to save their mama, Kenna folded it tightly into a square which she then placed into a cotton sachet to carry with her at all times.

That same eve was to be Karina's trial, not that she'd get anything of the sort, but as the girls dressed in their woolen cloaks and Jeremiah in his black suit and overcoat, a feeling of peace had settled over them all. It didn't take magic to know it was Karina's doing, for each of them started to hear her words within their minds. *'I'll be okay. Please do nothing to jeopardize yourselves."*

Kara and Kenna both pleaded with her to let them come save her, but she refused, saying she wouldn't allow them to face the same fate and would use every ounce of her magic to ensure it and that they just needed to trust her.

Jeremiah, Kenna, and Kara watched as Karina was dragged from the prison and into the courtyard, bound at the wrists. The waiting crowd hissed and cursed hatefulness upon her as she was led to the stake. It took everything within them to not smite them all in that very moment, but instead, they did as their sister asked, and remained patient. Once Karina was tied in place, the pomp and circumstance began.

Kara and Kenna wept as the announcement was made. "Hear ye, hear ye. We gather this night to present evidence of solid conviction upon this witch, Karina Howe. Her use of dark magic was witnessed by our own Governor Danforth and the accusing Ann Putnam."

They all gasped at the mention of Mrs. Putnam's name. Jeremiah pulled them close, wrapping his arms around them in an effort to comfort and calm.

"The devil's mark has been identified upon her and as the Court declares, 'Thou shalt not suffer a witch to live,'" the executioner declared. With no further words, the torch was cast at Karina's feet, and the crowd roared like zealots, cheering and excited for her death, but it was only when she smiled did a hush fall over the crowd.

Kara and Kenna stood hidden at the back of the crowd, silently pleading. *"Do it now! Use your magic to escape."*

They watched as she closed her eyes and began her chant. Magic built within them all, as they too, heard her plea. *"Come to me, death that be, flames surrounds, peace abounds; flesh to earth, spirit to soar, transport our souls, alive forever more."*

Bursting free of their mortal flesh, they all flew into the cosmos. Encased in fire and wind, their energy signatures spun wildly into the night sky. They could feel each other's magic sparking against one another and knew Karina's spell had worked. It wasn't until the final moment, before plummeting into their first lifetime, did they realize they had been separated from Karina. Their souls solidifying in their new bodies, and thankfully, Jeremiah was still there, as he promised, and they knew he always would be.

Arrived and checked into separate rooms, Caris and Kennedy unpacked, while Karina waited for Jason's arrival. They'd all determined it would be best if they held off until morning before starting their search for Ann.

"I'm here, babe. What room are we in?" Jason asked, holding his cell phone to his ear with his shoulder as he reached for his bag.

"501," Trin supplied.

"Great, see you in a few." Clicking the key fob, he set the alarm on his truck and entered the hotel. Ready to have his woman back in his arms, he made a bee-line for the elevator, pushing the button for the fifth floor with smile on his face.

"Well, well, I never thought it would be this easy to lure everyone out, and lookie here...just the man I need."

Jason spun, but not in time as a cloth settled over his nose and mouth. Sliding down to the floor he sent his last waking image into Trin's mind. The image of Ann Putnam's snarling face.

Chapter Twelve

"Damn that witch! This has been a trap the entire time," Trin cussed.

"Okay, okay, calm down," Kennedy instructed, using her FBI training to take control of the situation. "We're all upset, but losing focus won't help us find him any sooner." Kennedy kneaded a cotton sachet between her fingers which throughout the centuries had been the only thing that helped calm her usual hard-edge.

"Let's do another scrying spell and see if we can pinpoint her exact location now that we're in town," Caris suggested. Trin nodded but continued to pace while Kennedy set up the map. Taking point, Caris pulled her pendulum from her pocket and motioned Trin forward to join her. Using Trin's previous spell, Caris repeated, "Find the one we're looking for, Ann from now and before. Reveal to us what hides within, my Lord and Lady, let the search begin."

Unlike their previous attempt, their pendulums spun wildly, jerking and bobbing between multiple spots on the map. "What does that mean?" Kennedy asked.

"It means that Ann has figured out a way to access her magic, or at least some form of it. She's blocking us," Trin seethed.

"Shit!" Kennedy snapped, rolling her shoulders. "We have to do something else that will help pinpoint her location."

"Or maybe, we stop trying to find her and start trying to find Jason instead," Caris suggested.

"Yes! Brilliant! Let's do it." Kennedy rushed forward.

"Lord and Lady lead thy search, find our loved one who's in a lurch. Snatched out from our loving hands, show us his spirit upon this land." Trin focused her magic and love into the spell and gasped as their pendulums began to swing and sway. Then, unexpectedly, both crystal points started to glow bright blue, warming until they'd burnt a hole directly into the map.

"Yes!" Caris cried as the hole pinpointed Jason's location.

Trin sunk down onto the bed. "Oh no."

"What's wrong?" Kennedy asked.

"That's the location of my old house. Katherine

Hunniwell's home from 1702," Trin shook her head.

"Well, that can't be good, but I guess it's no surprise." Caris gathered the ruined map and tossed it into the trash.

"It does makes sense. If Ann is able to access her magic, she could have followed my energy signature, and it would have led her there. It's empty now, owned and maintained by the town, so it would serve as the perfect hideout," Trin explained.

"Well, what are we waiting for?" Kennedy slid her gun into the holster and nodded at her sisters. "It looks like it's old home week, and I'm ready to pay Ms. Putnam a visit."

The car ride was tension-filled as they made their way to Black Point Road. "Do we have a plan, or are we just lookin' to bust in?" Caris asked, finally breaking the silence.

"I'll do a scanning spell to confirm they're there, then we'll enter through the back door," Trin explained.

"Sounds good, but I go in first," Kennedy stated flatly, leaving no room for argument.

When they turned off onto Old Country Road, Trin motioned for Caris to slow the Jeep. "I just cast a dampening spell so Ann shouldn't be able to sense our approach. Caris, there should be a rough trail in the grass up here on the right. It will lead us to the back of the property."

"10-4," Caris smiled into the rearview then followed Trin's

instructions. Two minutes later, she parked the Jeep along the forest's edge and joined her sisters in the thick bushes surrounding them.

"Okay, let's go. I want to get a little closer before doing the scanning spell," Trin whispered. Creeping forward, she struggled to fight the memories pulling at her psyche, as images of Nadie and the other Native women she'd helped while here bombarded her mind.

"Are you okay," Caris asked, noticing the grimace on Trin's face.

"Yes. I'm just getting a bit overwhelmed with memories from my past here." Trin wiped her forehead. "I'll be okay. Here, this should be close enough."

Trin, Caris, and Kennedy stopped about twenty feet away from the back of the Hunniwell house. They crouched down behind a split rail fence, still hid by lush chokeberry bushes and the birch grove that surrounded the house. Trin looked at the tiny cottage, appreciating the bright red paint and all the upkeep and restoration that had kept her home standing strong for this long. There was no visible movement inside, but they'd know soon enough if they were truly alone.

"Do you need anything for the spell?" Kennedy asked.

"No, but I'd feel better if we joined hands," Trin smiled.

Clasping hands, they closed their eyes and let their magic flow together. "Give us sight to see this night, waiting within or on the run, show us the whereabouts of Ann Putnam." A golden light sparked between them, hovering and bobbing in the air within their circle before shooting off towards the house. Passing straight through a window, it pulsed within the space. Trin, Caris, and Kennedy could feel the magic throb within their chests, confirming Ann was waiting inside.

Kennedy nodded at her sisters then took the lead, pulling her gun from her holster, she crouched down and walked purposefully towards the back door. Trin continued to scan the area, making sure they weren't walking into a physical or magical trap of some sort, while Caris brought up the rear, clutching a bag of herbs and securing her poison ring onto her finger as she continued to chant protective spells under her breath.

Creeping up the single stone step, Kennedy eased the backdoor open, which to no one's surprise had been left unlocked. Talking into their minds, she sent her sisters a warning. *"Obviously, this is still part of her trap, so be careful."*

Trin pushed through the memories flooding her mind and scanned the main floor, desperate to latch onto Jason's energy signature. *"There!"* she thought. *"He's in the living room, just up ahead."* Trin pushed passed Kennedy, her magic surging through her veins and rounded the corner, ready to face their enemy.

"Trin!" Jason exclaimed from the chair he was tied to in the middle of the room.

"Are you okay?" Trin asked, rushing to undo the ropes.

Kennedy stood guard, aiming her gun at the main opening to the room. "Where is she?"

"Upstairs. She kept going up and down, muttering to herself about a new destination, but she didn't hurt me." Jason shrugged out of the ropes and stood, pulling Trin into his arms. "She's definitely crazy, though, and I have no idea what's she's talking about."

Trin looked around the familiar space and could no longer ignore the sinking feeling in her gut. "I think I do."

Caris walked forward, giving Jason a quick hug, then turned to Trin. "What do we need to do?"

"She's clearly regained use of her magic somehow, and by doing so, I think she's trying to go back to a time in which she had full access to her powers," Trin explained.

"Time travel? Are you serious?" Kennedy snapped.

"Yes, unfortunately. By kidnapping Jason, she knew I'd come here, I think she's trying to latch on to the magical energy left here from my previous life. You said it yourself, you don't know where you were during that time period, but she was with me here," Trin gestured around the room, "and I think she's trying to get back there."

"Damn! Well, then let's go stop her," Kennedy barked.

Trin and Caris nodded then followed Kennedy towards the winding staircase.

"Jason, you stay down here in case she gets past us," Kennedy instructed.

"Got it." Jason kissed Trin and gave her a firm, reassuring nod.

"Let's go," Trin instructed.

Ascending the stairs, Kennedy led the way, halting them halfway up. She pointed ahead of her to a red light, pulsing from the other side of the attic door. *"Caris, strengthen your protection bubble around us, now!"* Kennedy sent into her sister's mind.

"Goddess of love, Goddess of light, protect us with your awesome might. Within this bubble, we are safe, protected by your loving grace."

Nodding at each other, they continued up the stairs, listening as Ann's muffled voice became clearer and clearer the closer they got.

"Time is mine, fluid and true. Take me back, my curse to undo." The red light surged throughout the entire space as Ann finished her spell.

"Go, now! Stop her!" Trin cried.

Kennedy burst through the door, racing into the room and dove for the tail of Ann's dress just as she slipped through the portal hovering before them in the middle of the room "Dammit! What do we do now?"

"Follow her, we have no choice!" Trin leapt forward, diving through the swirling vortex and found herself flung out into the very same room. "What the hell?" She looked around, nervously, waiting for her sisters to arrive, which they never did. The portal snapped closed with a pop, leaving her standing alone in the familiar attic. She spun around, taking in the differences in the scene and sank to the floor. "Oh no. Goddess help me!"

A creak from the stairs pulled her to her feet. "Madame Kate? Is that you?" a long-forgotten but familiar voice rang out. "What are you doing up there? Did I forget something for dinner service?" Nadie climbed the stairs and gasped. "Madame Kate, what happened to your clothes, your hair? Have you been assaulted?"

Trin quickly gathered her wits. "No, no, Nadie. Nothing like that. I was just walking in the garden and snuck up here to retrieve a vase for the flowers I wanted to gather. You go on, now. I'll be down in just a bit."

Nadie's big, beautiful eyes narrowed as she contemplated her mistress's words. "Yes, Madame. But let me know if you'd like me to gather anything else from the garden." She turned and walked back downstairs, leaving Trin to collapse onto the dusty wood floor in despair.

Chapter Thirteen

After a fitful and well deserved cry, Trin pulled herself together and descended the stairs. She needed to find her sisters; she knew they'd followed her through the portal, even though they didn't emerge in the same place. Her instincts told her it was because they weren't previously a part of this time, but that wouldn't make locating them any easier. Trin just hoped they'd arrived in the same vicinity at least.

Pausing in the middle of the staircase, she listened for any movement below, knowing she'd need to get out of this house as soon as possible or risk running into the previous version of herself. Sensing the coast was clear, Trin eased down the last few steps and tiptoed across the foyer.

"I'll ask you again...what happened?"

Trin spun and found Nadie poised to strike with a machete in hand.

"Nadie..." Trin held up her hands, having no idea what to say since she hadn't pinpointed the timeline yet.

"I know it is not you, I can feel traces of the Madame in your veins, but you are not her. Explain." She raised the machete higher above her head, looking like a true Indian warrior.

Trin nodded, remembering the tribe's magic and wasn't surprised Nadie could sense hers. "I'll explain everything, but first we need to leave this place. Is there somewhere I can hide?"

After a few seconds of consideration, Nadie gestured out the back door but didn't lower her weapon. In a show of good faith, Trin led the way, exiting the house first. "Which way?" she asked.

"Towards the river," Nadie replied, solemnly.

They walked the half-mile trail through bushes, ferns, and trees without saying a word. At times Trin wondered if Nadie was even still there since nothing but the sounds of the forest and snapping sticks under her own boots rang out around them. A quick tug at her arm, however, confirmed she was. "Get down," Nadie instructed, pulling her to the ground and blocking her view.

Trin crouched silently and watched as Nadie surveyed the nearby riverbank with curiosity and a hint of fear. "Explain now," the Indian priestess demanded.

"You are correct; I am not the Madame Kate you know. However, I am the future version of who she becomes." Trin swallowed and eyed Nadie's weapon, hoping that wouldn't be the last sentence she ever muttered. "If you take my hand, I can show you." Trin extended her right arm.

Nadie cast another nervous glance at the river then placed her left hand in Trin's.

Visions of Trin's lifetimes and that of her sisters' flew between them in a rapid exchange, magic to magic, and truth to truth. She needed Nadie to understand that she wasn't here to alter the timeline, but to find her sisters and stop Ann from doing so instead. Settling on a particular memory of herself as Katherine, Trin felt the maiden's doubt lower as the vision of the two of them together, mourning the loss of Nadie's mother sank in.

Nadie's long braids fell forward as she knelt in front of Trin with the shimmer of tears in her eyes. "I understand. Your soul is pure and your memories of me are the same that I share of you. I will help you," she stated with a quiver in her voice.

"Thank you so much." Trin felt their past connection and pulled Nadie into a warm embrace.

"First, we need to get you and your sisters back to my

tribe. It will be the safest place for you to hide." Nadie stood and offered her hand.

"That's the thing, I don't know where my sisters are just yet." Trin shrugged and fought back her pooling tears.

Nadie smiled and pointed at the river. "I believe I do."

Trin stood up and followed Nadie's gaze. Caris and Kennedy were sprawled on the riverbank, wet and unconscious. *Oh, thank the Goddess.* Rushing into the frigid water, Trin splashed to the other side. Kneeling between them, she checked their pulse and threw herself atop them as they started to stir. "Thank the Goddess you're both all right," Trin sobbed.

"What happened? Where the hell are we?" Kennedy struggled to sit up.

"You are not in Hell, you are in Maine," a stern voice replied.

Kennedy looked up and gasped. "Who's the Pocahontas look-a-like?"

"This is my friend, Nadie. She is going to help us," Trin replied.

"It's my honor to help, but we must go now." Nadie held out a hand to Caris while Trin helped Kennedy to her feet.

"Follow me, and stay low." Nadie took off, scrambling up the muddy bank and continued into the forest. Large pines and a mix of birch and alder trees surrounded them. Trin, Caris, and Kennedy trailed behind with not nearly as much stealth. Thankfully, the small tribe was located in a small clearing just a mile or so into the woods.

"Wait here." Nadie crept forward with the grace of a cat, ducking into a small wooden frame house. The long rectangle base and arched ceiling seemed to be covered in what looked like woven mats and sheets of bark. Trin strained to listen as Nadie spoke in her native tongue, her voice steady and rising above the others when needed as they debated their future. Male and female voices joined, blending into a cacophony of loud buzzing, making it seem as if their lives were in the hands of a swarm of bees. Suddenly, all fell quiet as Nadie returned with a pile of skins thrown over her shoulder. "Put these on."

The sisters didn't ask questions but instead discarded their modern clothes and items, burying them beneath the nearest tree, and dressed in the native attire Nadie supplied. They stood still as she marked their faces with white paint and waited while she braided their hair and smudged their auburn locks with dark brown dye that smelled of barks, roots, and leaves. "This will allow you to blend in while you're here, but please don't leave the wigwam unless I say so." Nadie nodded swiftly, then without waiting for a reply, led them through her Indian village.

Tan faces peered out from inside wigwams as they passed. Multiple huts of varying sizes created a circle around a central fire pit that was the size of a small pond. Rocks lined the edges of the cooking pit that was dug deep into the ground. The only two Indians who acknowledged their presence were the pair of older women stoking the fire and tending what looked to be fish wrapped in seaweed.

"This is unreal," whispered Caris, clearly enamored by the history that surrounded them.

"You're telling me. The last time I wore a beaded Indian gown and moccasins was for a Halloween party back in 2012." Kennedy gasped in awe.

"Hush," Trin whispered.

"Through here, please," Nadie pointed at the rough-hewed door that marked the entrance to one of the longhouses located in the very back of the village. "You will be undisturbed as long as you remain inside. I'll return this evening with food and blankets, but you will be asked to help around the village as long as you're here. I'll provide your tasks tomorrow morning just after sunrise." Nadie nodded then immediately fled, leaving them alone to gather their wits.

"Where do you think Ann went?" Kennedy asked, sitting cross-legged on a grass bed layered with hides and furs.

"I'm not sure. We didn't find each other in this time until much closer to the end of our life spans here, and from what I can tell, that's still quite a few years away," Trin explained.

"Great. So not only do we need to figure out where *our* Ann is and what she's up to, but we also need to locate the Ann from this time, to make sure of what? That she doesn't take our Ann's place and race back to the future?" Caris shook her head. "I'm so confused."

Trin joined Kennedy on the bed and gestured Caris over, patting the space beside her. "Look, first of all we need to stay calm. If we panic in any way, it will jeopardize our safety here. We need to follow Nadie's instructions and help out where we're told, then, once the chores are done, we'll work here, inside the hut, to locate Ann. It's as simple as that."

"If it's so simple, then let's just find Ann right now and get out of here," Kennedy snapped.

Trin sighed. "I understand the urgency, but you have to remember, there's not just one version of Ann here so our spell will have to be crafted a bit more carefully than usual. Plus, we don't have access to a map, so I may need Nadie to retrieve my special scrying bowl from the house here and use a different technique for the spell." Trin reached for her sisters' hands. "Can you please just trust me?"

Caris and Kennedy both leaned into their big sister's embrace and conceded. "We trust you," Caris replied.

"Good. And to be honest, I'm not worried about running into the version of Ann from this time. She, nor I as Katherine, ever came into this village. So as long as Nadie and her tribe are willing to keep our secret and let us hide here, we should be safe from encountering the previous version of either of us, which is extremely important. And, I'm hopeful it won't take long to find *our* Ann, since you guys wound up so close and weren't even from this time originally. I think her portal may have had a bit of a range, but not much, so hopefully she's ended up in this same vicinity too. Tonight, when Nadie returns, I'll ask her if she's seen another new or strange woman in the area and we'll go from there."

"Sounds like a plan. Now how about we get some rest until she returns with some food. I'm beat," Kennedy pulled back and stretched her arms into the air.

"Me too," Caris moved to the bed on the opposite wall and settled in.

Trin eased off the bed Kennedy had claimed and walked to the next one just a few feet away. "Crazy how much a little time travel can take out of ya." Trin shook her head then eased onto the bed and settled into the warmth of the furs, praying silently that their plans would go smoothly as her mind drifted to Jason and just how hard this was going to be on them all.

Chapter Fourteen

All three sisters slept, albeit fitfully, until Nadie returned with their dinner of fish, clams, pine nut bread, and maple sugar sweetened tea.

"Please eat and rest. I'll return tomorrow morning with your assigned jobs. Good night." Nadie stoked the fire then departed in a rush, leaving Trin no chance to ask about Ann or the bowl she'd need to use for her spell.

"Well, crap. I guess I'll ask her tomorrow when she comes with news of our jobs." Trin sighed.

The girls just nodded then began to enjoy their dinner.

"This isn't so terrible," Caris smiled, appreciating their use of herbs and seasonings.

"Yeah, things could definitely be worse," Kennedy agreed. "How did you become so close with Nadie during your lifetime here? I thought this area was riddled with violence and raids during that period."

"Oh, it was. King Phillip's and King William's war decimated this area, but before the start of Queen Anne's war the colony was reoccupied. Even though my husband at the time fought viciously against the Indians of this land, I worked in secret with the native women and aided in their education. Many of the local tribes were taught to speak English as a way to smooth relations between our cultures," Trin explained between bites. "I just took that a little further and offered secret tutoring in my home that would expand their women's knowledge and therefore help establish the peace we all so desperately yearned for. We were all sick of seeing our men die." Trin shook her head and lowered her eyes back to her plate.

Caris and Kennedy shared a look of concern. "I'm sorry you suffered the loss of a husband," Kennedy offered. "I have to admit, I guess I never really think about all the baggage we've accumulated during our soul travel."

Trin shook off the memory. "It's okay. I tend to forget all the things I've seen and experienced as well. But knowing it is all a part of what led us to each other and to the gift that the Goddess bestowed upon us, I wouldn't change a thing, so please don't worry. I have no desire to alter this timeline or any other." Trin smiled at her sisters.

The girls relaxed while continuing to enjoy their simple meal when suddenly, the rhythmic beat of drums filled the air. Kennedy and Caris jumped from their beds.

"What's that. Are we in danger?" Caris asked.

Trin laughed. "No. Not at all. No one's declaring war. It's just their version of a rain dance."

The girls raced to the door of their hut, peering through the holes left between the timbers and the overlaying bark. Mesmerized, they watched the tribe, male and female both, dressed in beautiful skins and elaborate headdresses as they wove between each other in zigzagging patterns, tapping their feet to the rhythm of the drums. Their tribal song filtered up into the night sky, along with sparks from the fire created by something one of the elder men continually threw into the flames. The purple and blue smoke carried their intention towards the stars, creating a version of magic Caris and Kennedy had never seen before.

"It's like I can see the images of what they're asking for forming in the smoke," Kennedy whispered.

"Exactly. And now you know the other reason I got along so well with the tribe here. They carry a magic all of their own and recognized the spark within me as well." Trin smiled and joined her sisters at the door, grateful to witness the majesty of these people once again.

"It's so beautiful," Caris added, leaning against the door.

Suddenly, the flimsy door fell away and the sisters came tumbling out on the dirt. The drums stopped, and the entire tribe stared at the three impostors. Nadie raced forward as voices rose in their native tongue.

"Please, listen. They are my friends and are here only to help. They will be assigned work duty tomorrow, and you'll see, they will only lend strength to our tribe and bolster our magic. The elders have approved their stay, and they are to remain untouched," Nadie proclaimed.

Kennedy and Caris followed Trin's lead and bowed to the agitated crowd, then disappeared quickly back inside the wigwam, re-securing the stick-frame door.

"Dammit!" Kennedy cussed.

"I'm so sorry," Caris cried.

"It's all right, you heard Nadie; our stay has been approved by the elders. We just have to stick to the plan and everything will be fine," Trin said. "We'll accept whatever jobs they give us in the morning and do our best to repay them for their kindness. Then, once we're sure things have settled down, we'll get back to finding Ann and get the hell out of here."

Caris and Kennedy nodded, then all three sisters rushed back to their beds and listened as the drums slowly began to sound again.

SCARBOROUGH, MAINE
Present Day

"God dammit!" Jason cussed and ripped through the attic, tossing everything in his path as it became glaringly obvious that they'd all disappeared. Grabbing bowls, herbs, and anything else he could get his hands on, he looked for the tiniest of clues that would help him decipher where they could have possibly gone. So far, the only thing he found was a converging trail of footprints in the dust all leading to a single spot on the floor then completely vanishing.

"Come on, Trin. Where did you go?"

He continued his search until he heard the roar of an engine approaching the front of the house. Peeking out the attic window, he saw a service vehicle and busted ass to get downstairs and out the backdoor before he had to explain his presence here. He didn't think anyone would believe he'd been kidnapped seeing as the house was now completely empty.

Running out the back, he hurdled over the fence and dipped into the tree line. Catching his eye, he noticed something shiny from behind the bushes and was pleasantly surprised when he found Caris's jeep with the keys still in place. He flipped the ignition and backed down the trail until he came to the fork in the road. Righting the vehicle to face forward, he spotted the house's roofline just beyond the trees and immediately turned left, desperate to put some distance between him and the park ranger. Jason held tightly to the steering wheel, absorbing the bumps while travelling too fast down the dirt road. Soon, he hit asphalt and found a nice little pullout. Retrieving his cell phone, Jason punched open his navigation and searched for the hotel's address. Twenty minutes later, he arrived back at the scene where his troubles began. Checking at the front desk, he confirmed his and Trin's reservation and obtained a new key since his original had been waiting in the room with Trin. He also made sure to ask what their checkout date was scheduled for.

"We have you leaving us in three days, Mr. Hardy. Check out is at 11am," confirmed the hostess.

"Thank you." He turned away calmly, then made his way to the room he and Trin were supposed to be sharing. Looking at the adjoining door, he sent up a prayer to the Goddess that he wouldn't have to extend their stay. If that happened, he'd have to charge both rooms—his and Trin's, plus Caris and Kennedy's to his credit card. He shook his head; the money wasn't the issue, but trying to figure out how to keep them from wondering where his family was for three days or more...yeah, that wasn't going to be fun.

Chapter Fifteen

SCARBOROUGH, MAINE

1705

Soft rays of sunlight filtered through tiny holes in the ceiling and walls of the wigwam. Trin laid still, listening to the sounds of the forest waking for the day and knew Nadie would be arriving soon. Glancing at her sisters, she found peace in their sleeping faces and hoped she could pull them through this without any added stress. Easing out from under the furs and skins, she tiptoed from the hut, stretching in the brisk morning air and taking a moment to herself to cast her greetings to the Lord and Lady. "God and Goddess of the moon, stars, and sun, shine your bright blessing upon me as this new day has begun."

"What a lovely blessing." Nadie's soft voice drifted to Trin's ear like a feather gently floating on the wind.

"Good morning." Trin hugged her friend. "I'm terribly sorry for what happened last night. I hope our abrupt appearance didn't cause you any trouble."

"I may be bold, but I would have never brought you into the village without the elder's approval." Nadie smiled.

"Well, again, we can't thank you enough. I do need to ask you a question, though, before we begin our day."

Nadie nodded for Trin to continue.

"Have you seen any other strange women in the vicinity? As I showed you before, we are looking for the one who pulled us all here."

Nadie shook her head as she handed Trin a loaf of what looked and smelled like corn bread. "I'm sorry, but I haven't. Today will be the first day I return to the house to see the real Madame Kate, though, so I'll be sure to ask if she's seen or heard anything as well."

"Thank you. Also, I need to ask you for another favor. There is a bowl that's kept in the attic. It should be in the far back corner, wrapped in a painted deer skin. Could you please bring it to me tonight?"

Nadie tilted her head, contemplating her answer a little too long for Trin's liking. "I need to attempt a scrying spell, and unfortunately I don't have a good enough lay of the land to draw a map. That bowl has been in my family for a very long time," Trin confessed.

Nadie relaxed. "Of course, I'll bring it by with dinner. Now, here is another bit of bread for your sisters, and I have the jobs the council assigned to you for the day. *You* will aid our shaman with his healing, while your sisters will help attend the tribe's garden and retrieve the traps from the river."

"No problem. Where do I go to meet the shaman?" Trin asked.

"His hut lies another quarter mile down this path." She pointed to a thin dirt trail that left the village and veered further into the forest. "Now, if you'll wake your sisters, I'll escort them to meet the other women they'll be helping today."

Trin nodded and entered the hut, finding Caris and Kennedy already on their feet.

"Gardening and retrieving traps? Really? Why do you get the cushy magical job?" Kennedy teased.

"I'm sorry. Probably because I'm the only one here who she's witnessed using magic before. Well, not me, but you know what I mean." Trin shrugged.

"Yeah, we get it. But be careful, okay," Caris added, gratefully accepting the loaf of bread for her and Kennedy.

"I will, and you too. See you back here this evening." Trin pulled them both into a quick hug then led them outside where she waved goodbye to the three of them.

Realizing she had a moment alone, she returned to their hut and re-fixed her braids. Brushing as much of the grass and dirt from her dress as she could. She laughed to herself, thinking back to her previous life here and how many times she'd wished she could have tried on some of their beautiful clothes and furs. Now, she would give anything for a camera to capture the four of them in this lifetime together; her, her sisters, and the one Indian maiden who'd made her previous life here somewhat bearable and purpose filled.

Shaking the memories from her mind, she left the wigwam and ventured down the path towards the shaman's hut. Ten minutes later, she stopped dead in her tracks, staring at the most elaborate dwelling she'd seen so far. Hanging over the door were a large set of moose antlers, draped in beads, dried plants, and red-dyed leather ribbons. Encircling the base of the entire structure were the skulls of smaller forest animals; rabbits, fox, squirrel, and lord knows what else, all staring up at her with feathers sticking out of their eye sockets.

Trin shivered then eased towards the front door. "Hello? I've been sent from the village to help with your healing today," Trin called out, suddenly worried she should have brushed up on what she remembered of their native tongue. She was pleasantly surprised when a scratchy voice replied in clear English.

"Enter."

Trin ducked her head beneath the threshold and found herself transported. Not literally this time, but from the advancing world around them and back to a time filled with magic and the humble worship of the land and sea. Bones, herbs, feathers, and nets filled the hut, along with a thick layer of smoke, leaving Trin dizzy as her eyes and lungs fought to adjust to her new surroundings.

Blinking through a thick fog, Trin spotted the shaman to her right. He was sitting at the far end of the hut on a raised wooden platform covered with hand-stitched pillows, woven blankets, and layers upon layers of skins and furs thrown about in a hap-hazard way. His attire— comprised of much less—was nothing more than a breech-cloth made of tanned skin. Trin waited patiently for him to speak while taking in his wrinkled skin and wise eyes that matched his gravelly voice.

"Who said I needed help with my healing?" he asked, breaking their awkward silence.

"I was told by Nadie that it was my assigned tasked for the day. How may I be of assistance?"

The shaman squinted at Trin through the smoke, scanning her appearance from top to bottom. "You don't look like a maiden from our tribe. How are you supposed to help me?"

Trin lowered her head. "I'm not sure, but I'll be more than happy to try in any way you require."

After a few moments of awkward silence, he motioned her forward. "Join me." He pointed to a pillow opposite the small fire that burned in a large copper bowl set directly in front of him.

Trin bowed in thanks then took a seat, gasping when the old man blew a large plume of smoke into her face. Her chest constricted, pulling her stomach to her spine as a remnant of her astral self was yanked out her back. She felt it immediately; the shaman read her magical signature which now hovered directly behind her. She turned and gazed up at the hazy image of herself dressed in a puritan dress and dark woolen cloak, holding a wand high into the air.

"Seems like you'll be able to help me after all," he snickered.

Trin smiled and turned back to the tricky old man as her foggy form dissipated. She watched as he reached for another pinch of the fragrant tobacco he was smoking. "Would you like me to prepare us some tea?" Trin offered.

The shaman nodded. "But first tell me your name."

It was a simple question but one that held multiple answers. Should she default to her true name, knowing he'd seen her pure essence? Or should the life she was now living and would continue to be for the span of her magic remain the one she clung to? Or, should she use the name she was known for in this time? *Decisions, decisions.*

He watched her internal debate and eased her warring soul with one simple word. "Kanti." He pointed at her, nodding, then closed his eyes and took another drag from the long stem of his pipe.

Honored by her new Indian name, she smiled like a fool as she puttered around the hut, preparing tea and taking note of all the spices and herbs stored upon a raw wooden shelf. Returning to the platform she handed him a cup. "Do you have a preferred spice you take in your tea?"

He shook his head no then sipped the green tea, nodding in satisfaction. "Well made, now sit."

She dropped back onto the pillow, crossing her legs and awaited her instructions. An hour later, she woke from a deep meditative stupor she and the shaman had both entered and questioned if it had been intentional or not. She hadn't partaken in the pipe but thought perhaps he wanted a little more information on her before trusting her with his magic.

"We begin now," he stated just as a set of footsteps approached the hut.

Bells clanged from outside, and he motioned for her to greet their first client of the day. Trin, now Kanti, rose and started towards the door but stopped halfway there. "I feel I should know your name before we begin."

"You already do."

She closed her eyes and concentrated, pulling his name and a soul-deep connection from the journey they'd just shared. She smiled back at him and continued to the door. Easing back the bark covering, she welcomed a young man and his mother. "Aranck is ready for you."

Kanti stood off to the side while they spoke in their native tongue to one another. She could decipher a few words from their conversation that she remembered, but would wait for instruction before attempting to interfere.

"Kanti, please bring me a poultice of aloe leaves, bayberry root, and comfrey." Aranck instructed then returned to the conversation with his patients.

She'd been correct in her assumption; this particular poultice would treat a cut upon the boy's leg. Kanti mixed the ingredients in a wooden bowl with the hand-carved tools laying on the workspace just below the shelf. Adding in a bit more aloe, she released the soothing gel into the ground leaves which provided a nice binding agent. She turned to look around the space and spotted a skin hanging by the door. Bringing it with her, she returned to the boy and cleaned his cut with the fresh water it held, then applied the poultice and wrapped the wound with a strip of pressed cotton she'd found in the cubby next to the workbench. Looking up into Aranck's eyes, she knew what was expected of her next.

Laying her hands over the bandage, Trin summoned her healing magic and chanted under her breath as the shaman intoned his own rhythmic spell. "Goddess, heal this wound pure and true, aided by the love reflected in you. So mote it be." Her touch warmed, and the shaman smiled.

The young boy stood, putting his full weight on his leg and beamed at his mother. "Thank you," the woman repeated over and over as they left the hut, making sure to leave her offering of two polished stones and a sliver of bone in the bowl next to the door.

"Well done," Aranck stated as soon as they were gone. "I can see you're going to be of great use to us here."

Chapter Sixteen

"How was your day," Kennedy asked as she and her sisters fell into their beds back in the wigwam.

"Interesting. I was sent on a surprise soul journey, thanks to the tribe's shaman, then once he found me worthy, he gave me my Indian name. After that, I spent the day mixing poultices and healing tinctures for the tribe's injured and sick," Trin replied.

"Oooh, what's your Indian name?" Caris asked excitedly, pushing up onto her elbows.

"Kanti."

"Nice. I like it. Do you think we'll get names too?" Caris asked Kennedy.

"Who knows. Maybe after we pull more fish from the river or harvest more herbs from the garden they'll deem us worthy and give us a cool name too." Kennedy flopped over and faced the wall, pulling the thick blanket of fur up and over her head.

"What's the matter with her?" Trin sent into Caris's mind.

"She wasn't thrilled with our assignment, especially when the elderly women we worked with kept correcting the way she was collecting the fish."

"Oh man. Well, hopefully we can get some down time tomorrow and return before *Nadie leaves our dinner for us, so I can ask her if she's seen anyone else in the vicinity."* Trin shrugged, frustrated she'd missed her friend this evening.

"Yeah, I hope so too."

Trin smiled at Caris and watched as she tucked in for the night, then rolled over and silently cast one last spell before closing her eyes as well. *"The day is over, the night is here; please watch over all I hold dear. Let us wake to a brand new day, filled with joy in every way. So mote it be."*

Smoke drifted across the three sisters as they slept, bringing to life their dreams—or nightmares in the case of the youngest one. Aranck watched as images from Kennedy's dream took form in the fog; he watched as demons ripped apart her sisters and the loss had ripped apart her heart. She couldn't protect them before and was terrified she wouldn't be able to do so now.

He blew another burst of smoke into the room, shifting the vision to the middle sister's dream of a life with children. A large plantation with rolling greens and three sets of little feet padding next to their handsome father while she watched from the nearest bench. Suddenly, she grabbed her chest and screamed as her soul was pushed forward into her next life without warning.

The third puff of smoke fell over Trin, encasing her body in the magical mist. Images of her and her sister witches rose up from the wavering layer, dancing and frolicking along her body. A strong male appeared and whirled in behind her, grabbing her by the waist and bringing his lips to hers as they danced around a fire. The mist-made puppets twirled and spun as one big happy family until a dark ooze erupted from the fire and settled over them all. Aranck watched the foggy scene turn dark, the darkness blanking out the stars and coating everything in its path. The images of Trin, her lover, and her sisters melted into the ground, dissolving into nothingness.

The shaman blew out a cleansing breath then left silently, leaving the girls to dream in peace.

"What did you discover?" Nadie asked.

"Their souls are true and you're correct, full of magic. We

need them here," Aranck started back down the path that would lead him home.

"So what should I do about the bowl and the information the eldest wants from me?"

"Keep it from her," he simply stated then disappeared into the waiting arms of the forest.

Trin, once again, was the first one to rise. She tiptoed out of the wigwam to welcome the dawn of a new day but tripped over a wooden stake that'd been driven into the ground directly in front of their door. Reaching down, she retrieved a piece of thin parchment that was tied to the piece of wood. Scrawled in brown dye it read, *"Your breakfast will be brought by another. I will return soon – Nadie."*

Trin sighed, not happy with the feeling that was settling in her bones; Nadie hadn't brought her the scrying bowl she'd asked for, but also Aranck's words from yesterday had become a thorn inching its way further and further under her skin, *"I can see you're going to be of great use to us here."* That was the problem; they shouldn't be here and definitely couldn't stay.

"Good morning, Kanti. I'm Semcka." Trin stood to find another beautiful young maiden bowing in front of her. "Nadie instructed me to deliver your breakfast and your assigned tasks for the day." She handed Trin two more loaves of bread, wrapped fish, and two skins—one containing a batch of flavorful tea and the other, fresh water from the creek. "Your tasks are the same as yesterday, you with the healer and your sisters at the creek and gardens." Semcka smiled shyly then turned to leave.

"Wait. Can you tell me where Nadie's gone?" Trin asked, her question secretly carrying multiple concerns.

"I'm sorry, I do not know." Semcka skittered away, fueling Trin's rising concern.

Trin shook her head and re-entered the hut. "Breakfast is served."

Caris and Kennedy had nothing to add to the non-existent conversation as they ate, so after finishing, they sent Trin with the skin of water, while they set out towards the river once again with the skin full of tea. "Do you think we should say something to her tonight?" Kennedy asked Caris.

"What would you say?"

"Why the hell are we still here doing these stupid jobs instead of looking for Ann? That's what I'd say," Kennedy whispered.

"Then no, I don't think you should say anything. I'm sure

being back here is hard for her, and I know she already has Nadie gathering information and the things we need to cast our spell, so I suggest we just stay patient," Caris replied.

"Right. Patient while I pull stinking, flopping fish from the traps while you get to sort through the herbs and daisies in the garden, and Trin gets to use her magic to help heal people. Okay. I'll be patient." Kennedy tossed her braids behind her back and walked ahead.

"Hey! Stop complaining. At least we're safe here and not prisoners or worse." Caris caught her by the elbow. "Besides, you can work in the garden today if you'd like. I don't mind gathering the fish."

Kennedy let out a frustrated breath. "Okay, thanks. And, I'm sorry. Being here may be emotionally stressful for Trin, but I'm starting to feel weird too. I'll be happy when we can get out of here and return home."

"I know. Me too." Caris pulled her little sister into a quick hug then continued down the path toward the river, while Kennedy veered right toward the gardens.

Once she received her instructions, Kennedy settled in and began harvesting row after row of turnips. Digging in the dirt wasn't much fun either, but it beat dealing with fish traps and the woman who'd rode her ass about every single mistake she made.

"You look lost," said a soft voice.

Kennedy looked up into a set of large, almond-shaped eyes. The maiden was younger than Nadie and wore a plain skin wrap-skirt and vest, draped with a heavy fur instead of the decorated dresses she'd seen on the older woman of the tribe. "You could say that." Kennedy smiled.

"If you'd like some help, or some company, it would be my pleasure," offered the maiden.

Kennedy would much rather complete her task alone, but thought better of sharing those particular thoughts. She didn't know the customs here and wouldn't want to offend anyone by refusing their generosity. "Of course. Thank you. I'm..." Kennedy stopped, not sure whether to use her real name or if they should have received or even made-up names of their own by now.

"You're Ketnu. At least that's what my mama told me." She pointed to a woman a few rows away who smiled and nodded kindly.

"Yes, that's right," Kennedy agreed without hesitation. "And what's your name?"

"I'm Tawni." The young woman beamed, dropping to her knees and digging her hands straight into the dirt. It was obvious she was happy to help, but probably more so just to have someone to talk to.

Ketnu watched the sun cross the sky as she and Tawni talked all afternoon. They'd discussed the tribe's education and why everyone here was taught to speak English—for the furtherment of the trade agreements with the white men; how they were almost done with the food preparation and stocking up their winter stores—which Ketnu and her sister were currently a part of; and the arrival of Commander Nicholson— which was good news according to Tawni.

"Thank you for letting me help today." Tawni threw her arms around Ketnu/Kennedy's waist then raced off to help her mother home.

Kennedy walked down the path back toward the river and met Caris at the fork with a smile on her face. "Hi!"

"Hi. It looks like gardening agrees with you," Caris teased.

Kennedy shook her head and took her sister's hand. "Yes, I guess it does. And how was your day?"

"Not bad. I think I finally got the traps down now, and a woman gave me my Indian name today."

"Hey, me too! I'm Ketnu? What's yours?" Kennedy asked.

"Karoot." Caris laughed.

"I guess that's fitting, seeing how you're a genius at plants and herbs," Kennedy said, lowering her head. "I'm sorry I took your spot in the garden today. I know it's where you'd be more comfortable."

"It's okay. I really didn't mind working at the river." Caris nudged her sister's shoulder as they entered the village.

They received a few waves from some of the other women

they'd worked alongside, as well as some admiring looks from a few young tribesmen. They smiled and laughed, waving back and feeling less stressed until the moment they saw a white woman entering the village. Gasping and rushing for their hut, they prayed Trin would return soon without running into the previous version of herself currently milling about.

Chapter Seventeen

Caris and Kennedy peered out from behind the door of their wigwam, monitoring and keeping tabs on Katherine Hunniwell as she moved throughout the village, shaking hands and handing out gifts of some sort.

"I thought Trin said she never came to the village during her lifetime here," Caris stated.

"I thought so too, but there's no doubt that that is her. Katherine was the only white woman close to the tribe here." Kennedy shook her head and took a deep breath. "This is bad. It means things are changing."

Caris didn't respond and both girls fell silent, returning their attention to the commotion outside. Suddenly, the strange yet familiar woman stopped and looked longingly into the forest—exactly in the direction Trin was set to come from when returning from the shaman's hut.

"Shit! What will happen if Trin sees the older version of herself?" Caris gasped.

"I'm not sure, but she made it pretty clear it's something we should definitely try to avoid." Kennedy spun and began searching frantically for anything she could use as a distraction.

"Wait! Come here, she's leaving." Caris waved Kennedy back toward the door.

They watched in silence as Katherine waved goodbye then turned back down the path that would take her home. "Thank the Goddess." Kennedy pointed to the shaman's trail where they watched Trin peek out from behind a tree then race toward their wigwam in a mad dash.

"Oh thank goodness you made it!" Caris threw her arms around Trin's neck.

"What happened? Do you know why she was here?" Trin asked.

"No. We were just returning to the village when we heard a few raised voices and then looked up to find her passing out gifts and talking to some of the tribe. How did you know she was even here?" Kennedy asked.

"I felt her, and unfortunately, I think she felt me too." Trin started to pace the length of the dirt floor.

"I think she did too. We saw her look down the path you were on like she knew something or someone was there." Kennedy dropped down onto her bed. "I thought you said you—*she*, never came here?"

"She—*we* didn't." Trin raised an eyebrow. "And did you notice the bruises on her face? I never had those in my time here."

"No. What does that mean?" Caris whispered, dreading the answer.

"That I was right," Kennedy sighed, "things are starting to change, and we need to get out of here as soon as possible."

Trin looked around, noticing no extra bowls and dropped her head. "This is exactly what I feared, and to be honest, I think it's just the beginning."

"What do you mean?" Caris gasped.

"I mean...I think there are far worse consequences headed our way." Trin lowered herself onto her bed, sitting cross-legged with her back against the cold, hard wall.

"Like what?" Caris pleaded.

"Well, I'm not sure about either of you, but I don't exactly feel up to par at the moment. At first, I thought it was the stress of everything that's happened, but now, I'm not so sure." Trin stated.

"What do you mean? What else could it be?" Kennedy asked.

Trin dreaded having to say it out loud, but knew she couldn't deny it for much longer. "I think being here is causing my powers to weaken."

"WHAT?" Kennedy flew from the bed as Caris started to cry.

"Calm down, please." Trin begged. "I need time to assess everything, but what I can tell you is when I lived here before it was without you both, so my magic was diminished. And yes, we are all here together now, but I'm not sure if that trumps the timeline of my previous life or not. Like you said, it's all very confusing, and if we're going to stop Ann, we need to be at our best. I suggest we all get some rest until Nadie returns, then I can question her and we'll go from there. I need to know why Katherine ended up in this village today, seeing as it was the first change I've noticed, I think it's somehow important."

Caris wiped her eyes and nodded, trying her best to follow her big sister's lead and remain calm. She crawled into bed and attempted to control her soft sobs as Kennedy continued to pace.

"We need to test our magic now," Kennedy demanded.

"And what if something goes wrong?" Trin asked. "What if because we aren't as connected here as we were at home, our magic is skewed and we alert Ann to our whereabouts? What then? We'd be sitting ducks just waiting for her to come and send each of us to a new timeline, truly tearing us apart for good." Trin closed her eyes and let her head fall back onto the bark-covered wall. "I will not rush things because of fear or anger, so you're going to have to trust me to get us through this." She opened her eyes and pierced Kennedy with a determined gaze. "And I promise, I *will* get us through this."

Kennedy's jaw ticked as she contemplated Trin's words. It wasn't that she didn't believe her; she knew her sister would move heaven and earth to keep them safe and make this right, but she had to admit, patience wasn't exactly her best virtue. "I believe you, and I do trust you. I just want you to trust us too. We can help, and you need to let us." Kennedy returned Trin's stare. "You may have been alone when you were here before, but you're not alone now. Don't try to take this on all by yourself. Promise me."

"I promise." Trin offered her sister a slight smile then crawled into bed and forced herself to relax. Taking deep, steadying breaths, she guided herself into a meditative state, hoping the Goddess would answer her call and help provide the answers she needed to get them out of here and safely back home.

SCARBOROUGH, MAINE
Present Day

After using his magic to gain access to Caris and Kennedy's hotel room, Jason gathered everyone's things and loaded up his truck, securing the tow-strap between his back bumper and the front of Caris's Jeep. It was going to be a long trip home, slow and go, and he had no idea what to do about Kennedy's work car. His only choice was to leave it in the hotel parking lot and hoped to hell that she could deal with it once she got back. He hoped no one would call it in, because that would open up inquiries as to why she was here and where she'd gone, and those weren't questions he could answer. At least not without magically interfering with the memory spell she'd previously cast, and that was never a good idea.

"Yes, please charge both rooms to this card." Jason handed his credit card to the twenty-something receptionist behind the hotel counter and sighed. He hadn't seen nor heard from Trin or her sisters in the three days he'd remained in Scarborough. It was time to return home and hopefully use all the tools at his disposal to find a way to reach them.

"Here you are, sir. All set. We hope you enjoyed your stay." The receptionist smiled and recited her rehearsed line then returned to her computer work.

Enjoyed my stay...not exactly.

Chapter Eighteen

Gliding through the astral plain, Trin focused on the center of her magic and called to the Goddess. *"My lady, please guide me through this unknown time, protecting and preserving what's truly mine. Help me return us to the present day, thwarting all evil along the way. So mote it be."*

The sound of tinkling bells woke Trin from her meditation, and while they weren't a response from the Goddess, the peaceful feeling they elicited brought a smile to her face.

"Good morning," a soft voice greeted.

Trin sat up and watched as another unfamiliar maiden entered their wigwam and headed straight for Kennedy's bed.

"Tawni? What are you doing here?" Kennedy asked, pushing out from underneath her pile of fur blankets.

"I made you something." The young maiden handed Kennedy a beautifully beaded headband. The shells and beads were the colors of the sea: blue, white, and gray. There was a large silver conch with bells, feathers, and dyed leather strands attached to the side that would hang down perfectly along her braid. "It's lovely." Kennedy smiled and smoothed her fly-aways then slipped the gift onto her head.

"You look so beautiful." Tawni beamed as she reached up, gliding her fingers along Kennedy's braid. The look of longing on her face spoke to the notion of *the grass is greener on the other side*, or *always wanting what you don't have*. "I wish my hair was red like yours," she confessed a moment later.

Kennedy scooted from the bed, shooting Trin a knowing look that they'd have to recolor their locks later today to avoid any further notice. "Thanks, but I prefer it dark. Would you like to help me dye it again later?"

Tawni's eyes lit up and Trin smiled, happy Kennedy successfully diverted the conversation to avoid Tawni pointing out any other *differences* between them. "Yes, please!"

Kennedy laughed as she slipped her moccasins on then pulled out the rest of the leftover bread and tea from yesterday's dinner. "You're here pretty early. Have you eaten yet?"

"No. I wanted to get here before you left to give you your present, and I wasn't sure if I'd see you in the garden again today or not." Tawni shrugged and smiled shyly, finally noticing Trin and Caris in the room. "Hi! I'm Tawni."

"So we've heard." Caris laughed and gave the young maiden a wave. "Your gift is lovely."

"Thank you. I thought it would help hold Ketnu's braids in place while she worked."

Trin's eyes snapped to Kennedy's. *"Ketnu?"* Trin questioned into her mind.

"Yes. Sorry, with all that happend last night, we forgot to tell you. We received our tribal names yesterday. I'm Ketnu and Caris is Karoot."

Trin smiled and nodded her head, then turned her attention back to their young visitor. "Tawni, would you happen to know where Nadie is?"

Tawni stiffened and stood up, leaving her clump of bread on the plate. "No. I'm sorry. I don't know." With the nervousness of a rabbit, she bolted toward the front of the hut. "I hope to see you at the garden again today, Ketnu. And I hope you like your gift." She spun toward the door and was gone in a flash.

"What in the world was that?" Caris asked.

"I'm not sure." Kennedy popped the piece of bread into her mouth.

"Well, something's not right. That's the second person who's run away from me when I asked about Nadie." Trin huffed.

"That's no good. Do you think we should go look for her?" Kennedy asked.

Trin took a deep breath and walked to the small fire in the center of the room. "Let me question the shaman today, but if I get the same sketchy response, let's plan to head out this evening and see what we can find."

The girls agreed and finished their breakfast just as Semcka arrived outside their hut to provide their assignments for the day. Accepting the same old, same old, Trin nodded and headed back down the path that would lead her to Aranck's, while Kennedy and Caris returned to the river and garden.

"Do you mind if I return to the garden today," Kennedy asked, "I want to see if I can get any more info out of Tawni."

"Of course. I think that's a good idea. She seems to have really taken a shine to you." Caris wrapped an arm around her sister's shoulder.

"I don't know about that. She's sweet, though. Her mama is the one who told her my name yesterday. I had no idea," Kennedy shrugged.

"Your favorite lady from the river came up and practically slapped me on the back and announced I'd been named Karoot, then walked off without another word." Caris shook her head and laughed. "That one definitely needs to work on her bed-side manner."

"No kidding. Well, hopefully now that we've received our names, we've graduated to some level of acceptance, however small it may be." Kennedy shrugged off Caris's arm and gave her a wave goodbye, turning up the path to the garden. It was her hope that she could take advantage of that *acceptance* and get the info they so desperately needed.

"Ketnu!!" Tawni shouted as she rushed over, clearly thrilled with her arrival and acting as if they hadn't just seen each other minutes ago. "Hi! I'm so glad you're back. Do you mind if I help you again today?"

Kennedy looked into the girls expectant eyes and couldn't help but smile. "Of course. If it's okay with your mama, that is."

Tawni turned back to her mother whose kind face and agreeable nod sent the girl fluttering even closer to Kennedy's side. Their morning was spent pulling more turnips and talking about the boy who'd helped Tawni gather the beads and shells for the headband she'd made. "He's really sweet and I think we would be a good match. At least that's what my mama says, but we have to wait and see what Papa thinks and if the elders will approve." Tawni wiped her brow, finally taking a breath between sentences as she plucked the last vegetable in the row.

"Looks like that's it for the day." Kennedy stood, stretching her stiff legs and back.

Tawni pushed up from ground and looked at their designated section and beamed at their progress. It was barely past mid-day and they'd completed their task in record time. "Since we're done early, would you like to help me gather some more items so I can make gifts for your sisters as well?"

Kennedy contemplated Nadie's original instructions about staying inside unless they were helping the tribe, but after receiving their names and working together for the last few days, she didn't see the harm in taking some extra time to help her new friend. Besides, it would give her the alone time she needed to ask some questions. "Sure, that sounds fun."

Tawni ran to get her mother's approval then led Kennedy down another path that sloped away from the opposite side of the garden towards a small grove of birch trees. The yellowing leaves and white bark confirmed a change in season was upon them, punctuated by a crisp bite of wind as they made their descent. Kennedy pulled her furs tight around her shoulders and began her interrogation right away, not sure how much time they'd have before needing to head back. "Do you come out here often?" she asked.

"As often as I can. I love it here. The trees really speak to me." Tawni's eyes were glazed over with affection and Kennedy suddenly wondered if she really *could* communicate with the trees in this grove. Kennedy watched closely as she bent down and sorted through the underbrush for seeds, nuts, and any other shiny nuggets she could find.

"How do you turn them from their natural state into the beautiful colors you use in your gifts?" Kennedy asked, gently laying a hand on her headband.

"Magic!" Tawni's eyes lit up, and once again Kennedy was left unsure whether she was being literal or not. However, before she could raise another question, Kennedy's chest tightened in a painful pinch. Grabbing her heart, she pressed at the sinking feeling that had penetrated bone deep. As she struggled to catch her breath, she looked up the path and found it blocked by three of the largest trees she'd ever seen. Each had to be more than two-hundred feet tall and at least one-hundred feet around. They were connected at their base by large knuckles, each trunk baring a split where the bark was peeled back in layers—splits that seemed to be pulling at Kennedy's very soul. The splits looked like doorways into another realm, and the fact that magic tingled along her skin the closer she got, left her undoubtedly shaken. "We should go back." She grabbed Tawni's arm.

"Why?"

Kennedy had to think fast. "Because, I can feel the air changing and don't want to get stuck out here in a storm." She ran her hands up and down her arms, shivering to give her words more validity and impact.

"Okay. But if we finish early again tomorrow, will you come back with me to look for some more stones?" Tawni asked.

"Perhaps." They continued in silence, walking back to the garden then down the other path toward the village. Kennedy bid farewell to Tawni and raced for her hut. She paced and pondered what their next move should be while waiting for her sisters to return. It was early evening before Caris and Trin joined her in the wigwam. By then, she'd become a completely frazzled mess.

Chapter Nineteen

"We have to go, now. I'm telling you, there's something about those trees, and I think it has to do with Ann. I'm sure of it!" Kennedy smoothed her hands over her unbraided, frizzed-out hair.

Trin followed her sister's footsteps that had become worn in the dirt while contemplating what she'd described. "Three trees, each split to its core and radiating magic?" Trin repeated out-loud.

"Yes. Exactly," Kennedy snapped.

"Okay. I agree. Let's go check this out, and hopefully, we can sneak close enough to the Hunniwell house to look for Nadie as well. I'm pretty sure she's been holed-up there, and I'd really like to ask her why?" Trin explained.

"What did the shaman say today?" Caris asked as she pulled on her moccasins.

"He was no help." Trin quirked a brow. "He likes to talk in riddles, or at least that's what they sound like to me. Every time I'd ask about Nadie, he would just spout some nonsense and change the subject."

"Well, let's go. I want to know what we're up against." Kennedy pulled her thick fur covering over her shoulders and walked out the door.

Caris reached for the small skin bag that previously carried their breakfast. Dumping out the crumbs, she replaced them with some stones and herbs she'd gathered earlier today, in case they needed to cast a spell once they arrived at the trees.

Trin placed a hand against her chest, letting the magic of the bone talisman she'd made earlier in the week radiate under her touch then followed her sisters outside. The night was chilly but not completely unbearable. Trin pulled her furs snug and tilted back her head, enjoying the stars as they twinkled against the black blanket upon which they lay. The sound of their footsteps were muffled against the thick layer of moss and pine needles that coated the ground. She followed Kennedy and Caris down the path they'd become accustom to, happy they'd each found their place within the tribe as she had.

"This way," Kennedy motioned up the hill toward the garden.

The air smelled of cultivated dirt, and Trin smiled in appreciation of the organized rows of vegetables. The proficiency of the tribe was something she appreciated, not just from their current experience, but from her time spent here in the past. The gatherings and teachings she'd arranged as Katherine Hunniwell were some of her favorite memories from that particular lifetime.

"Down here," Kennedy prompted as she veered down the hill on the other side of the garden. The path sloped slightly, leading them straight into a small grove of birch trees; their white trunks and yellowing leaves created a welcoming sight.

Shuffling the last few feet, Caris stopped and bent over. Placing her hands on her knees, she started to heave, struggling to calm her suddenly heavy breaths.

"Car, what is it?" Kennedy asked, rubbing her sister's back.

"I'm not sure," she gasped. "My chest just got tight all of a sudden, and it became hard to breathe." She inhaled deeply and stood upright, arching her back while pressing a hand against her breastbone. "I'm okay now, let's keep going."

Kennedy eyed Trin, sending her next thought into her sister's mind. *I think you better scan the area for magic. Whether it's Ann or something lingering from the tribe, this place definitely has a pull.*

Trin nodded and obliged silently. *"Show me now, the lay of the land. Magic fingers from a mysterious hand. Reveal to me the sight I need, to protect this land and us sisters three."*

Trin stepped in front of her sisters and held out her arm, blocking them from the path ahead. The forest shifted from dark to light, as if the landscape had just undergone an x-ray. Trin could now see streams of white energy pulsing from where each of the sisters stood, running along the ground as if marking a runway. Following the line that radiated from beneath her feet, Trin walked forward to the base of the adjoined cluster of trees. The three portals—and that was definitely what they were— were exactly as Kennedy described them. Large trees connected at their bases, each split wide by the magic held within.

"They are portals," Trin motioned Caris and Kennedy forward, "and each one holds a different magic, connecting them to a different time." She followed the pulsing lights at her feet to the center tree, lifting her hand and pushing against the magic radiating from its core. Kennedy's line led to the tree on the left, and Caris's to the right. "I think we're each supposed to go through our assigned one."

Kennedy's head snapped to Trin. "Assigned by who?"

"I'm not sure. It could be the magic of the tribe, or the Goddess giving us directions, or on the negative side of things, it could be Ann trying to pull us apart. I simply don't know."

"I'm not blindly walking into a time-shifting portal without knowing who the heck's behind it." Caris's voice held an edge of panic, one which they all seemed to be sharing.

"I agree, and that's not what I'm suggesting." Trin reached for her sister's hand, hoping to reassure her in this unsure situation.

"I think we should..." Kennedy's words cut off and her eyes filled with terror as an invisibile force pulled her through her designated portal.

"No!" screamed Trin, reaching for her sister just as two small pops split the air, yanking her and Caris into their respective trees as well.

BLACKBROOK, NEW YORK
Present Day

"What the hell!" Jason yelled as what looked to be a disheveled Indian maiden materialized in the center of the sacred circle he'd just cast. He'd been attempting spell after spell to locate the girls for the past week, but then suddenly—before he could even intone his latest chant, a stranger popped into existence inside his very home.

Collapsing to the floor, the woman held up a hand. "J, it's me." Kennedy looked up and met his gaze, sucking in deep breaths as she adjusted to the wave of nausea time travelling had brought on.

"Oh my God, Kennedy, are you all right? Is Trin all right? Where's Caris?" He raced to her side, kneeling down and placing a hand on her back while continuing to scan the room.

His frantic questions and rapid movements forced Kennedy to close her eyes as she fought the dizzy spell threatening to overtake her. "Give me a few, please." She eased further onto the floor, rolling over until she was curled into a ball. "Time travelling sucks."

Jason tried to hold his tongue, wanting to give her the space she needed, but unfortunately, time was not on their side—this, he could feel all the way to his bones. "Where have you been, and were Trin and Caris with you?"

"Yes. After we followed Ann through the portal in Maine, we ended up in the same area, just three-hundred years earlier."

"Holy shit! Are Trin and Caris still stuck there, or are they following you back through?" Jason scanned the room again, hopeful the love of his life and her sister would appear in front of him at any given second.

A slight shiver shook Kennedy's exhausted frame. "I don't think they're coming."

Caris screamed as an invisible forced yanked her through the tree on the right and straight into the portal waiting within. Moments later, she snapped into existence and found herself in an all too familiar place. Large, crocodile tears streamed down her face as she looked around the small cabin where she and her sisters had been born and raised.

"Kara, is that you, my child?" Her mama's voice sounded from the back room, bringing on another round of sobs and stalling any words she tried to form.

Her mother, alive and well, peeked out from around the corner and smiled, not even flinching at Caris's odd garments or haphazard appearance, or the fact that she was at least fourteen years older than she should have been in this time. "I've been expecting you," her mother stated, coming into full view and opening her arms wide.

Caris didn't question how she'd known she'd be coming, or whether this was some kind of twisted time-dream replay, no, she simply ran into her mother's waiting embrace and cried her heart out.

"There, there. Everything will be all right. You're safe, and we have all night to get to work. We'll get you back there, and in doing so, save your sister as well."

Trin didn't fight the invisible force tugging at her heart. She simply closed her eyes and let destiny pull her forward through the portal of the center tree.

Feeling a cool breeze upon her face, she opened her eyes and looked up at the Hunniwell house in its original state. Her *husband's* voice echoed from within, and Trin watched as three silhouettes paced back-and-forth behind the windows on either side of the front door.

"They've been at it for awhile now," Nadie's soft voice drifted from just over her shoulder.

Trin took the time to really look at her beautiful friend and realized this version of the Indian maiden was from their current visit to their village, not the version true to this time. Trin's attention snapped back to the front door as the original Nadie burst from the house and raced into the forest.

"How did you get here?" Trin asked.

"I assume the same way you did. I was pulled through the center tree in the birch grove. Its magic called to me and once I was close enough, I couldn't stop myself," Nadie explained. "I'm sorry. It's why I've been missing. I've been stuck here, watching as history changes itself."

Trin gasped. "What do you mean, changing itself?"

"I'm sure you remember, we were never caught by Mr. Hunniwell in our true time here. This is an alteration and one that may not end well for either of us."

Trin looked back at the house just as a *smack* and a scream rang out from inside. *Ann's trying to get me killed*, her subconscious supplied. "We have to do something! Will you help me?" Trin asked.

Nadie squared her shoulders and nodded in response. "Just tell me what to do."

Chapter Twenty

BLACKBROOK, NEW YORK

Present Day

Changed and fully rested after a good nights' sleep in her own bed, Kennedy joined Jason in their workspace downstairs. "Have you found a way to re-open the portal?" she asked, getting straight to the point.

Jason wiped his brow then continued to crush herbs beneath his pestle. "No. Not yet."

Kennedy dropped her head and joined him, silently organizing all the oils and candles he'd laid out to anoint. There wasn't much else to say; they had a job to do and they both knew it. She understood that while he was happy she'd returned safely, the fright of what could be happening to Trin and Caris temporarily overshadowed that joy.

"Could you hand me some of that peridot?" Jason asked.

Kennedy reached for the tiny glass bottle and smiled at the beautiful green stones held within. She removed the miniature cork stopper and shook out a small handful into her palm. "Peridot," she peered into his mortar, "combined with Anise. Smart!"

"Thanks. I'm hoping the peridot will do its job to destroy the negative magic I can feel emanating from the energy of the portal, and the anise should help us focus our astral bodies during the trip back."

"Excuse me?"

"What? Did you expect me to just sit here, waiting to see if Trin and Caris eventually pop up? You know I can't do that." Jason released the pestle, it's loud clank punctuating his frustration. "I thought it would be wise to send our astral bodies through first to see where we're going to end up and if Trin and Caris are even close by. I wasn't planning to just step through into the unknown."

Kennedy held up her hands. "Like I said, it's smart. I'm just surprised you want to go. I thought the level-headed Officer Hardy would choose to stay behind and maintain a secure perimeter for when we all returned."

Jason stopped, mid-step and stood silently at the point where the portal's magic still pulsed in the air. "I just can't sit here and do nothing."

"Then don't. Go back to Maine, see if you can find Ann in *this* time—hell, I'll go back with you, but jumping straight through another portal doesn't seem like the best idea." Kennedy shook her head. "I'm sorry, Jason, but I really think we should both stay here."

Jason's chest rumbled as he tossed the contents of his mortar onto the ground, scattering the peridot shards across the floor. "Fine. We'll stay here."

IPSWICH, MASSACHUESETTS
1685

"Now, Kara. It's time."

Caris, grown and transplanted back to her childhood home, followed her mama's instructions and tossed the olive branch onto the ritual fire they'd built at their sacred space in the woods. Sparks shot into the air, drifting up into the night sky.

"Repeat after me," her mother directed. "Time is mine, fluid and true; transport me back to the world of new. Please reunite my sisters and me, as I will it, So Mote It Be."

Caris repeated the chant three times and gasped when a shimmering green orb took shape above the fire. Through it, they could see her current home and standing within it, Kennedy and Jason. Caris turned to her mama with tears in her eyes. "I wish we had more time."

Her mother hugged her tightly and kissed her wet cheeks. "So do I, sweet girl, so do I. But you must go. This is the only way, and remember what I told you."

Caris nodded, and after blowing a kiss to the woman who'd meant the most to her in the entire world, she leaped into the portal, emerging on the other side into a plume of green dust.

BLACKBROOK, NEW YORK

Present Day

Lifting her foot, Caris plucked crushed shards of peridot from the rough underside of her moccasin and squealed when Jason and Kennedy swept her up into a massive group hug.

"You're safe! Thank the Goddess," Kennedy whispered as they held each other tight.

"Yes. I'm fine, but Trin is not. We have to go back!" Caris pulled from their embrace with tears in her eyes.

"What do you mean? What's happening to her?" Jason demanded.

"Ann has trapped her in her past life in Maine—the original one, and has altered the timeline which has put her in danger."

"How do you know all this? Is that where your tree took you too?" Kennedy asked.

"No." Caris shook her head. "The only reason I know is because of ..." Caris swallowed past the lump in her throat, "Mama. She saw it all."

Kennedy's small but confident frame shuddered, requiring Jason to catch her before she collapsed to the floor. "You were sent back to Mama?"

Caris nodded. "Yes. She said that she'd seen all of this unfold in her visions, and that we were the only ones who could save Trin. You, me, *and* Jason."

Jason looked between the girls. "How am I supposed to help? I was going to stay here and return to Maine to try and find Ann in this time like we'd discussed."

"Oh, we're returning to Maine, it's the only way to access the portals again. But you have to come back with us," Caris demanded. "Mama saw it. You're the only person who can set the timeline straight."

Jason took a deep breath and straightened his shoulders. "I'll do whatever it takes." He hugged Caris and Kennedy, then they all dispersed to their individual rooms, rushing to pack for their impromptu trip back to Maine. Kennedy, and now Caris, knew exactly where the split-tree portals were located, and with any luck, they'd make it there before nightfall.

Jason sat in the back of the Jeep, silent and understandably focused. He had prepared by dressing to match the girls in the native clothes they provided, and tried to remain serious as they'd marked up his face with tribal paint. He looked like an Indian warrior with feathers stuck in his hair and a machete at his side. "Do we know where this portal will spit us out exactly?" he asked, finally breaking the silence.

"Yes, it will place us outside the Hunniwell house in Trin's original lifetime there," Caris stated, but said nothing more.

His personal firearm sat in his lap, unloaded of course, but the cold metal provided an anchor for him as he ran his thumb up and down the barrel. "Did your mother explain how I'm supposed to fix the timeline?" he asked.

"Yes. But your gun won't help you." Caris lifted her eyes to the rearview mirror and shook her head. Clearly, she didn't want to talk about this now, and Jason supposed there was no point. He'd said it himself; he'd do whatever was necessary to save Trin and knew the girls would too.

"Did Mama say if Ann was there, and if we'll encounter her then, or does that happen back here, at home?" Kennedy asked.

"She didn't say. Only that we had to restore the timeline in order to save Trin. Now enough with the questions, I don't know everything so stop asking." Caris reached for the knob on the radio, turning the volume up and bringing their conversation to an end.

Chapter Twenty-One

Kennedy was bounced awake and found herself back where all this had started—Scarborough, Maine. Caris was driving down the hidden path that would once again lead them to the back of the current Hunniwell property. "Wow. That didn't take long." She sat up, rubbing her eyes.

The Jeep was quiet as Caris whispered to her sister, "After we park, it should be just a quick jaunt over the river and through the woods to..."

"Grandmother's house we go?" Kennedy teased.

"Haha," Caris replied dryly.

Kennedy laughed and turned back to wake Jason.

"I'm awake," he stated flatly, determination shining in his eyes.

They rolled to a stop and parked the Jeep in the same place as they had before. After assembling the few items they'd planned to take along, Caris locked the rest of their belongings inside and hid the keys under a nearby rock. "What? I don't want to risk losing my keys in 1703." She shrugged in answer to her sister's questioning gaze.

"Good idea," Jason added. "Now let's just hope *we* don't get lost in 1703."

Kennedy stayed quiet and the mood remained somber as they started their trek back towards the river. It was strange seeing the same terrain they'd just left not more than two days ago in such a modern and manicured state. She hoped things hadn't changed so much that they couldn't find their way back to portals, but if what Caris said was true, their Mama still saw the trees standing in the same location today. Kennedy sighed and looked ahead at her sister leading the way. The idea of Caris getting to spend time with their long-passed mother pulled at every emotion she carried within her: love, heart-ache, envy, anger. If only her path had led to the right tree instead of the left. A smile lifted her lips as a random thought drifted to the forefront of her mind. *Maybe after all this is over, I can use the right portal and go back to see Mama myself.* Thunder rolled as she finished the thought.

"Come on, we're almost there. It's just up over this hill and down the path," Caris explained. Jason nodded and gripped the weapon at his side. He was nervous, and rightfully so, Caris thought. It was going to be hard to explain that his sole purpose here was to kill a man in cold blood. Caris shook her head and trudged on, carrying the weight of the future with her.

Originally, Richard Hunniwell was killed in an Indian raid at the river behind his home. But, since Ann had altered the timeline, she put Trin and all the Indian women she'd helped in serious danger, which Caris was sure was her full intention. Not to mention the danger of how his continued influence could affect the outcome of the war. When they got there, she'd have to tell Jason the truth and hope to hell he'd follow through or else all would be lost.

"Car, it's this way." Kennedy interrupted her internal dialogue, ticking a thumb in the direction of the path she'd ventured off.

"Yeah, sorry."

Kennedy eyed Jason who just shrugged and trudged on. Moments later, they arrived at the trees. They were just as Kennedy remembered and hoped Caris had a plan to access the magic they'd need to activate the portals. Kennedy gasped. "What if the portals have moved?"

"What do you mean?" Caris asked.

"I mean, before the center tree is the one that led Trin to the time she's currently trapped in, but what if for some reason, that's no longer the case. What if we go through that same portal and end up somewhere else entirely?"

Jason's head dropped back with a huff. "Yeah, this is helping my confidence," he stated sarcastically.

"I'm sorry. I just don't want us to be caught off guard. I think we should test the portals," Kennedy suggested.

"How?" Caris asked.

Kennedy looked around, then asked, "I don't suppose either of you brought your phones?"

Jason nodded and reached into the skin pouch slung around his waist. "I did."

Kennedy grabbed the cell and opened the camera, sliding the setting to video. "Car, pull a string from the hem of your dress."

Caris did as her sister asked then handed her the thread. Kennedy quickly tied it around the phone and held it up in the air. "Once you activate the portal, we'll send this through and pull it right back to see what's been recorded."

"That's a good idea if it works, but I'm not sure it will, considering the energy involved," Caris replied.

"Only one way to find out." Kennedy wagged her eyebrows.

"Do you know how Trin activated the portals last time?" Caris asked.

"I think she did a scanning spell, but maybe it was her magic that triggered the trees. I'm not really sure." Kennedy shrugged.

"Okay, no more guessing. Let's do this!" Jason clapped his hand in a wide arc.

Kennedy pressed play on the video recording as Caris stepped towards the center tree and transformed her mother's recent words to meet their current needs. "Time is mine, fluid and true; take me back to this land once new. Please reunite my sisters and me, as I will it, So Mote It Be."

The center tree sparked to life, sending its bright green light surging from deep within its split center. "Throw it now," Caris yelled.

Kennedy tossed the phone into the crack, waited fifteen seconds, then yanked it back.

Rushing to see the recording, all three gathered around the tiny device. Kennedy pulled up the video and hit the play arrow.

"Oh no!" Caris's eyes bulged as the screen filled with Indian women running from the Hunniwell house in the distance. "We have to go now!" Grabbing their hands, she didn't wait for a reply, but simply yanked them into the pulsing portal.

SCARBOROUGH, MAINE

1703

Jason, Kennedy, and Caris—dressed in their native attire, crouched in the tall grass surrounding Trin's house from her former life.

"What do we do now?" Jason asked.

Taking a deep breath, Caris turned to face him. "Jason, I have to tell you something." She swallowed hard. "You have to kill Richard Hunniwell to set the timeline straight again," Caris explained in a rush.

Jason sank further onto the ground. "What? I don't understand."

Caris laid a hand on his shoulder. "If you want to save Trin and our entire future, you're going to have to come to peace with this, Jason. There is no other way."

Dropping his head between his knees, he mumbled. "I'm not sure I can do that."

Kennedy and Caris sat quietly while he contemplated this devastating news. Lifting his head, he met their concerned gazes. "I'm an officer of the law for goodness sakes. How am I willingly supposed to commit murder?"

"I know, and I'm sorry. But Mr. Hunniwell *will* kill Trin and all the women she helped if you don't do this. You have to dispatch him in order to save Trin and keep history as it should be."

"You make it sound so cut and dry. What if he fights back, what if there are others around who defend him?" Jason shook his head, expressing his concerns on a frustrated sigh.

"There won't be anyone else around. And we'll help you." She nodded toward Kennedy who had frozen at Caris's announcement.

"You'll just need to wait at the river and attack him once he enters the water. Use the machette and do it quickly."

"How do you know he'll go to the river now that the timeline has changed?" Kennedy asked, breaking her silence.

"Because, we're going to lead him there." Caris met her sister's gaze and the unspoken seriousness of the situation passed between them. They would gain Mr. Hunniwell's attention, marking themselves as targets, and lead him to the river to meet his fate.

Silence hung in the air for a beat until they all shifted and wordlessly accepted their roles. Reaching for each of their hands, Caris intoned another chant. "Lord and Lady watch over us all, and help us fulfill destiny's call. Setting time back on its course, requires action without remorse. So Mote It Be."

"So Mote It Be," Jason and Kennedy repeated.

Chapter Twenty-Two

Jason gave the girls a clipped nod and headed towards the river, while Kennedy and Caris started towards the house.

"Do you have a plan for us?" Kennedy asked.

Caris shook her head. "I don't think we really need one. As soon as he sees us he'll want to kill us, so all we really have to do is run."

"Wow. That's comforting." Kennedy huffed.

"It *will* be a comfort when everything is back to the way it should be and we've all returned home, safe and sound."

"You're right. I'm sorry. I know it must have been hard for you to keep what you knew from Jason. That was rough."

"Yes, it was. But Mama foresaw it, and I knew there was

no other way," Caris whispered. "He'll do what needs to be done."

Kennedy bit her lip at the mention of their mother and continued to creep forward toward the quaint farmhouse. "Do you know if Trin's inside?" she asked.

"I can't be sure, but I think so. The last image Mama saw was Richard hitting her."

"What? He's already hurting her?" Kennedy's voice rose with her anger, hardening her steps and her heart.

"Yes. Just like Ann had planned."

"Screw this! We want him to chase us right? So let's get on with it." Kennedy squared her shoulders, and cupped her hands to her mouth. Sucking in a deep breath, she let out a loud warrior's call, filling the twilight sky. "Iiiieyeyeye...."

Lights immediately flickered on in the Hunniwell home. "That did the trick. Get ready to run," Caris stated.

The girls stood proud and strong in their deer skins and face paint as Richard Hunniwell burst out through the front door with his musket in hand. He spotted them immediately and took aim.

"Get down!" Kennedy grabbed Caris's hand and yanked her to the ground.

Boom!

Peeking past the tips of the tall grass, the girls took off running towards the river as their enemy reloaded his musket.

Glancing back every few seconds, Kennedy quickly realized Richard Hunniwell was a pro killer. It only took twenty seconds for him to reload—powder, ball, wadding, ramrod then another *Boom* sounded as a lead bullet whizzed past their heads.

"Come on, hurry, we're almost there," Caris cried.

Cresting the hill, Kennedy searched frantically to locate Jason. "There!" Spotting him, she waved her arms in the air, then pulled Caris to the other side of the river, standing ready for Richard's arrival on the scene.

Mr. Hunniwell appeared moments later and stomped into the water, red-faced and out of breath. Their eyes met as he worked to finish his next reload. "You won't escape me, savages!" he screamed. "My wife has led you to believe that you deserve more than you do, but just like her, I'll quickly teach a lesson of what you deserve."

That did it. Jason crept towards his target, regretting less with every step. Using the river's gentle hum, he silently stalked around Richard's back and with a soul-deep sigh, he struck, quick and true.

Thwack. Richard's eyes grew wide as a small stream of blood seeped out the corner of his mouth. Dropping his gun, he fell face first into the river, exactly as history had planned.

Caris and Kennedy raced forward, hugging Jason as they all shed unabashed tears. "Let's go save Trin," Jason said, sniffling and wiping his eyes.

Hand-in-hand, they trudged out of the water and walked down the hill, easing up to the back door of Trin's past home.

Jason twisted the knob and stepped inside.

Trin's soft sobs sounded from the back room. The girls raced forward, not caring if anyone else was here and alerted to their presence. Kennedy called out, "Trin, it's us. We're all here."

Footsteps raced across the wooden floor and the bedroom door flew open. Trin wiped her eyes and threw herself into her sister's waiting arms. "Oh, thank the Goddess. I thought he was going to kill me."

"It's okay, baby. He can't hurt you anymore." Jason moved past the sisters and gathered Trin in his arms. He kissed the top of her head and held her tight as she let the stress of the situation leak out from her soul.

"Trin, is there anyone else in the house?" Kennedy asked.

"No. He killed two of the women upon his return; Nadie barely escaped."

"Where is the other you—the Katherine from this time?" Caris asked.

"The Nadie you know was brought here through the portal tree too; she and I snuck in after Richard left to hunt for the others. She took Katherine and hid her in the forest while I assumed the role and tried to work out a plan. Neither the true Nadie or Katherine are aware of our presence here."

171

"Good. Then let's find and flag *our* Nadie, because it's time to go. We've taken care of Richard," Caris stated with a grimace.

Trin nodded and hugged Jason tight, not needing any further explanation.

"Have you encountered Ann through any of this?" Kennedy asked as they walked out the back door.

"No. Have any of you?" Trin looked between her sisters and Jason, their collective nods tainting the mood even further. "Well, I have no doubt that since this little scheme of hers didn't work, we'll be seeing her soon enough. She won't give up."

"Good! I don't know about you, but I'm ready to get this over with and get the hell out of here," Kennedy spat.

Agreeable mumblings filled the space between them as they all padded quietly toward Nadie's hiding place in the woods. Trin's hands lightly skimmed the tops of the dried stalks that swayed at their passing, while rabbits and squirrels scattered at their approach. Stopping short of a tight cluster of low-hanging evergreens, Trin cupped her hands to her mouth. "Coo-coo" she softly mocked, watching the horizon for Nadie's signal that all was well.

A raised hand and a responding *"coo-coo"* confirmed Nadie would return Katherine to her home and inform her of her husband's death, setting history back on its proper course. Trin and Nadie had pre-planned all this, of course, and the next step was to wait for Nadie at the portal-trees. Together, they would all return to the current time and their lives within the tribe. After that, Trin, Caris, Kennedy, and Jason would solely focus on locating Ann and returning home.

If only things were that easy, Trin thought.

Chapter Twenty-Three

"Stop!" Nadie warned as she joined them on their approach to the portal trees. Dropping to the ground and crouching low, she listened to the wind and scented the breeze. "We're being surrounded."

Trin, Caris, Jason, and Kennedy pulled tightly together, back-to-back and readied their defense. Grasping hands, Caris muttered a protection spell under her breath. "Goddess of old, Goddess of new, protect our souls, through and through. Be with us on this day, so that we may return unharmed in any way."

A pack of seven Iroquois women crept from the forest, their axes and knives held high above their heads. Trin, however, was less concerned with them and more distraught at the vision of Ann Putnum in all black, slinking towards them from behind the trees.

"Figured we'd be seeing you soon," Trin spat.

"Yes, well, I didn't put much hope in that buffoon, Richard, to get the job done," her snarl morphed into a sickening smile, "that's why I brought reinforcements."

The cluster of female warriors took a step forward in unison, tightening the circle surrounding the group.

"Typical. Can't win the fight on your own so you cheat and align yourself with others," Kennedy's nostrils flared as she huffed and squared her shoulders.

"Yes. Exactly. My master taught me well."

"Oh, are you talking about the master we obliterated? Heinrich? Quick reminder, he's dead." Jason hoped his words held true and this whole time-travel fiasco hadn't resurrected that damn demon as well.

"Yes. That may be true, but the lessons I learned while in his service live on." Ann casually glanced at her fingers, picking and plucking at her black nails that had become unnaturally long and sharp—an obvious sign of the dark magic she'd been attempting to use. Gathering her tattered dress, she moved towards the group, stirring up dark shadows that radiated from her body. Trin noticed and quickly warned the others.

"Did you see that? It's as if she's cloaked in darkness and that does not bode well," she sent into their minds. *"Keep her talking while I prepare."*

"I assume your reason for all this is to gain your powers back, but if that's the case, why are we here? Hadn't you already achieved your goal back in our present day?" Caris asked, hoping Ann would start monologuing like most bad-guys do.

Ann scoffed. "Tools, ingredients, and borrowed powers? No thank you. That's all anyone can achieve in that time, but I will regain my true power, and in doing so, destroy you and yours." She raised her hands to the sky, casting the dark shadows high into the air. A swirling cloud of ominous proportions began to form, appearing as vicious as the tribeswomen who started to push forward again. Trin took a moment to look around the circle, staring into each of their eyes and was shocked by her discovery.

While appearing to be Iroquois with shaved heads and decorated ponytails, their war-painted faces couldn't hide the truth of their origin. These weren't native women; they were Caucasian and struck a remarkable resemblance to Ann.

"You found them." Trin focused her gaze back on Ann, pulling her attention from her current spell.

The storm died down and Ann's eerie smiled confirmed Trin's discovery. "Yes. My bloodwork, and all that testing and research paid off. And now, I only have two more to go, which is why I've brought you here." She gestured to the portal trees looming behind her. "I need your help and you're going to give it to me whether you want to or not."

Ann's sisters pressed their weapons in on Trin's group, thrusting them forward and closer to the trees.

Ann began to pace in front of the three splits that contained the portals. "You see, my problem is, I've only been able to come and go between our time in the present and this one. I'm sure it's thanks to your energy being the catalyst I needed to open the portal to begin with." She nodded at Trin. "And it would seem that energy remains the tie between the two." She shrugged nonchalantly. "The small amount of power I've obtained isn't enough to break that link. However, I know for a fact that you three can activate the other portals which will allow me to truly go home and save my two sisters who died before you cast your stupid spell in the first place." Ann's smile turned vicious as she chewed on the end of one of her tainted claws. "Then, once my family is reunited, I'll be able to regain my full powers and stop you from ever ruining our lives."

"And how do you know your plan will work? If finding your sisters is supposed to unlock your powers, then why aren't you stronger already since you're surrounded by seven of them in this very moment?" Caris taunted.

Ann's arms flew wide then smashed together in front of her as she finished in a dramatic clap. The ground shook as a small split opened up just in front of their feet. "My powers have grown since I found my sisters. But just like you, they won't be fully restored until our entire family is reunited," Ann explained with a disgusted leer.

"I don't remember your other sisters having power in our original lifetime. How is it that you're changing that now?" Jason asked, genuinely curious.

"With help, of course."

Trin's magic had almost reached its peak when Ann's words knocked them all for a loop. Suddenly Trin's mind was bombarded with questions from her family.

"Is she talking about Heinrich?" Kennedy asked.

"Will the demon be alive again back then?" Caris questioned.

"Well, shit! What do we do now?" Jason inquired.

"I don't know," Trin spoke aloud, answering them all at once.

"Enough! Let's get on with it, shall we?" Ann snarled and nodded fiercely at her sisters. Their blades nudged Trin and her family forward, edging them to the base of the trees.

Trin could feel the magic of the portals pulling at her and had to think fast. The idea of Ann returning to their true time was not only a bad idea in and of itself, but changing history to where the Putnam sisters *all* possessed magic, yeah...that was something they needed to avoid at all costs.

Trin quickly spoke into Caris and Kennedy's mind, *"Ground yourself in the here and now. Reach for the thread of the tribe's magic and hopefully we can alter the destination of the other two portals to mimic the center one. That will lead us right back to where we started, regardless what portal we step through. And keep your eyes open, we don't want to tip Ann off that we're casting a spell."*

All three girls took a deep breath and allowed their energy to flow from their feet and into the ground. The cold feel from the top layer of frost hit them first, then the warmth of the underlying soil as their tendrils of energy penetrated the earth. Pulsing currents of golden magic fed back into them as they latched onto the tribe's magic that had been engrained into the land, all while remaining unseen by Ann and her sisters.

Trin pulled the essence of the center portal to her through the roots of the tree, flaring feelers out towards Caris and Kennedy. Each quickly snagged at the root-line and drew it into their own web. Now, all connected, the girls pushed a surge of magic back into the ground towards the trees, shifting and changing the portals to all work as one.

"Let's go!" Ann spat, yanking at Trin's arm as she walked them towards the far left tree. "Wait thirty seconds, then follow us through," Ann instructed her sisters.

Not being privy to the girl's little alteration, Jason jerked against the blade that was digging into his back. "Let me go through with her," he demanded.

"Sorry, loverboy, you'll have to wait your turn," Ann mocked.

"Honey, don't worry, I'll be right back. Trust me." Trin sent her thoughts into his mind and gave him a quick wink.

Jason backed down but remained on high alert. Not sure what was going to happen but determined to not lose the love of his life for a second time this month, he nodded sharply and crossed his arms in frustration waiting, but ready to act.

Trin let Ann drag her forward and push her through the portal, almost bursting at the seams with laughter when they emerged right back where they started, in front of their families.

"What the hell?" Ann screamed.

"I guess you were wrong. Seems we can't open the other portals like you thought," Trin taunted, hoping she'd buy her fake excuse.

"We'll see about that." She nodded at her sister who had Caris lined up with the other portal, digging the tip of knife into the flesh of her shoulder blade.

Trin winked at Caris then stood silently as they popped out of sight and reappeared in the next second, emerging from the center tree.

"God dammit!" Ann screamed.

The three-ring circus, or more accurately, three-tree circus continued until every single one of the girls plus Jason had been ushered through all of the portals, each time returning to the same spot.

With a dramatic flare, Ann threw her hands in the air and the ground shook as snow spit from the sky like shards of glass, pelting only the girls and Jason. "Fix it! Now!"

Jason, Trin, and her sisters all shielded themselves from the elemental fit, casting a protective bubble around themselves that diverted the storm with ease. "Fix what? It's not our fault your magic isn't what it needs to be to pull this off. Guess you'll just have to wait until you're stronger and try again," Trin taunted.

"Oh, don't you worry about me. I'll definitely be back, and when I am, it will be the end of you and your family." With her ominous words hanging in the air, Ann snapped her fingers and disappeared with her sisters in tow.

A bank of fog crept across the forest floor in retreat as Caris huffed, "Um…well, I didn't see that coming. I didn't think her magic was that far advanced yet."

"Shouldn't we go after her?" Jason asked ready to put the time-meddling witch down.

"Not yet. We now know her plan is to gather her sisters and alter the origins of our past." Trin shook her head, deep in thought but clearly not ready to share all she was contemplating.

"Fine, so we know her plan, but how are we going to stop her?" Kennedy pressed.

"Wait, isn't that just what we did? Stop her, I mean." Jason questioned. "With the portals not working, we should be good, right? Won't that keep her from returning to our original time?"

"The portals aren't working because we have a hold of the tribe's magic and altered their destinations. That hold will dissipate as soon as we leave this forest, but hopefully Ann bought the ruse and won't come back to try again any time soon," Trin explained.

"Hopefully...but what if she does?" Kennedy sighed.

"Then I guess we all head back to Salem, back to 1693 and stop her from ever starting this chaos to begin with." Trin turned to Nadie who'd stood as a silent witness under guard by Ann's sisters. "Are you all right?" Trin asked.

"Yes. Your magic is strong and worked well." She lowered her head and kneaded the beads hanging from her belt between her thumb and forefinger. "But there's something I need to tell you."

Chapter Twenty-Four

Trin, Jason, and the girls listened as Nadie explained about the tribe's shaman wanting to keep them all there. "He asked that I keep the items you asked for from you, which I wasn't planning to do by the way, but then I got pulled through the portal and couldn't get back on my own. I'm so sorry."

Trin hugged her friend, leaving her arm wrapped around her shoulder as they walked back toward the village. "Thank you for telling me, but I'd pretty much figured it out on my own when he kept refusing to tell me where you'd gone, or why he wouldn't let me borrow any of the items from his hut. He's been very vocal about his gratitude for all the work I've done for the tribe, admitting he couldn't perform the same level of healing if it wasn't for my magic. It doesn't take a genius to figure out that he wouldn't want that to end."

"So you're not mad?" Nadie asked.

"No. I'm not mad. But as you well know, there's no way we can stay here, especially with Ann on the move." Trin smiled as she turned back to her sisters. "Thank you for trusting me today and pooling our magic. It seemed to be exactly the type of grounding and connection we needed to boost our strength. I could feel my magic surging, so hopefully, the next time we run into Ann, we'll be able to overtake her and her horde easily."

Caris grinned and moved to hug her big sister. "You're welcome. It was a good plan and worked like a charm. And I think you're right," she turned back to the group, "not only do we have to trust each other, but trusting ourselves to be a part of a greater whole is exactly the ticket to maintaining our full magic."

"Okay, yes, you're right. I could feel the Goddess's approval as we pulled together and let our magic weave the necessary outcome," Kennedy admitted with a lighthearted shrug.

"Well, good. Then we're all on the same page and on our way back to normal." Trin winked. The group stopped short as they entered the village. "Okay, well maybe not *exactly* back to normal." Trin laughed as they took in the entire tribe readying for a celebration. Indians covered in decorated skins and elaborate headdresses danced around the firepit, while a few of the tribeswomen worked to remove the wrapped seafood for a clam bake.

"Oh my god, that smells so good." Jason took a big wiff and moved toward the food but stopped short when he was halted by a spear and a harsh voice.

"Stop! Who is this outsider?"

Trin rushed to his side but had no idea what to say. Thankfully, Nadie stepped in and saved them all once more. "This is Kanti's mate...Jacwen. He's travelled far to meet her here and was attacked on the way. He has killed the Indian Killer, Richard Hunniwell, and should be welcomed and honored."

Jason bowed his head as he was inspected from top to bottom. Splatters of blood still marred his skin and arms from the strike that took Richard's life, which in this case was a good thing.

One of the elders pushed forward, waving a rattle in the air. "You are welcome here, Jacwen. Your body and spirit are strong. Feast, rest, and allow your soul to be renewed."

Jason flinched as liquid from the elder's rattle splashed across his face and torso. He hoped it was water but wasn't about to make a scene to find out. "Thank you. I am humbled by your kindness." Jason bowed low and melded back into the crowd with Trin, Caris, and Kennedy. "That was awkward."

"Not as awkward as it could have been if they hadn't accepted you," Kennedy stated.

"Too true." Jason turned to Nadie who remained close to their group. "Was Richard's nickname really *Indian Killer*?"

She shook her head yes. "He has been a blight on our existence since arriving on our lands. His wife," she nodded at Trin, "however, is the main reason we're still here and as well educated as we are. There are no amount of gifts that can honor or repay her for her sacrifices."

"Sacrifices?" Caris pried.

Trin shook her head ever so slightly, interrupting the conversation. "It doesn't matter," Trin said, her voice sharper than intended.

"You may not think it matters, but it certainly mattered to us." Nadie laid a hand on Trin's shoulder. "Your choice to stay here on your own as a single widow was a huge sacrifice, and I know it wasn't an easy one for you to make. Especially after your cousin arrived."

Caris, Kennedy, and Jason's heads snapped in Trin's direction.

Trin sighed. "I'm grateful my presence here helped the tribe, and I wouldn't have had it any other way, despite what my cousin had wanted. So again, it was no sacrifice. Establishing the Daughters of Maine was one of my greatest accomplishments while here." She clenched her jaw and shook her head at her sisters and Jason, hoping to make it clear she wasn't going to discuss this any further. Instead, she let the tribe's celebration absorb her and their problems for the night.

Trin woke the next morning to rain splatter on the thatched roof and snuggled deep into Jason's arms under the furs covering their bed. "Sounds like we better bundle up today. Winter's moving in," she whispered.

"Can't we just stay here, warm in each other's arms? I've missed you," Jason cooed as he pecked her cheek with tiny kisses.

"I would love nothing more, but I would prefer it if we were in our own bed, in our own time," she shifted to look him in the eyes, "wouldn't you agree?"

"Of course I agree, but no matter where we are, regardless of the time or space, I will never tire of having you in my arms." Jason kissed her softly and relaxed back against the grass-filled mattress.

"Oh my god, I love you both, but I just might gag if I have to listen to any more of this lovey-dovey nonsense," Kennedy teased.

Trin and Jason laughed then rose, leaving the warmth of their bed behind as they pulled on their moccasins. "Fine, fine. Then let's discuss what our next step should be," Trin suggested, arching her back and stretching her arms high into the air.

"Actually, I was thinking about something Nadie said." Kennedy shifted forward, sitting cross-legged on the ground as she re-braided her hair. "You made it clear you didn't want to talk about the sacrifices you made by staying here in that lifetime, but I think we should talk about when your *'cousin'* arrived. I'm assuming that was Ann, right?"

"Yes. But she didn't arrive until much later, so honestly, her presence here didn't impact my decision to stay as much as you think." Trin shrugged.

"That may be, but my concern is, if Ann was here with you in that time, what if *our* version of Ann went to find her older self in effort to alter things even further," Kennedy explained.

"Great!" Caris snapped as she flung herself from her bed. "Just what we need, another enemy to deal with."

"No, no, calm down," Trin stated soothingly, "like I originally stated, it's highly unlikely that's the case or else she would have already done it by now. She stated it herself, her attempt to use Richard was just a lure to get us to the portals, so if she did have the other Ann available to use against us, I think she would have played that card already."

"I agree," Jason piped in, "but why don't we just go back to our past and put a stop to all this. You said it yourself, if she succeeds we'll have no choice but to return to 1693 and stop her there. Why don't we just get a jump on that and head back now?"

Trin lowered her head as everyone waited for her response. She wasn't ready to tell them how visiting here had begun to affect her, and how she had no doubt it would only get worse if she were to travel to yet another time in their lives when she, Heinrich, and Ann were still connected by the demon's bond.

"It's my hope that we can stop her here. I don't want to travel back in time any further than necessary. Caris has already seen Mama and can attest to how that changed the course of things during that time. And while yes, we made adjustments to deal with those changes, we have to ask ourselves, what if we're not able to do so again? What if Ann succeeds in altering our past to the point where we have no future? Are you truly ready to take that chance?"

Footsteps crunching against the frost-covered ground outside broke the thick silence hanging in the air. "Excuse me," Nadie interrupted, poking her head in through the door. "There will be no assigned chores today, as today is a day of rest and reflection after last night's celebration." She entered the wigwam and walked straight toward Trin, handing her the baskets containing their breakfast. "I've also brought you this." She smiled shyly and pulled a smooth wooden bowl from the bag hanging at her hip. A split ran down one side that had been filled with crushed amethyst, the purple stone radiating light and magic that yanked Trin straight into a memory from another time.

IPSWICH, MASSACHUESETTS
1685

"Karina, could you please bring the mortar and pestle and join me in the back room?" her mama called out.

"Comin', Mama." Trin walked into their work space and gasped. "What happened?"

Her mama didn't respond but slowly turned and took the tools from her hands, dropping two small chunks of amethyst into the bowl. As she began to grind the stone into powder, she chanted—low at first but louder with each turn of her wrist. "Fill the crack in time and space, bind the bowl and mend with grace. Traces of me and my daughters three, bonded through time, so mote it be."

"So mote it be," Karina repeated sealing the spell. "What

happened to the scrying bowl, Mama?"

"I broke it and as you can see, it's now been fixed so that it may continue to serve its purpose for our family." She turned to face Karina, placing the now repaired bowl in her cupped hands. "This bowl will remain with you and your sisters for all time. It is just one of the tools that will help you in your future endeavors. Be sure to look for it in whatever time or place you may find yourself." Her mama ran a hand down her smooth cheek, and looked upon her with such love as only a mother could.

"Of course, Mama, I'll always keep it safe."

Chapter Twenty-Five

SCARBOROUGH, MAINE

1703

"Thank you, Nadie. As always, your help is very much appreciated." Trin smiled warmly and reached for the precious scrying bowl.

"For you, Madame, anything." Nadie bowed her head and exited the hut.

Trin turned to her sisters, beaming. "Okay, we've got work to do, but first, do either of you remember any other tools like this bowl that Mama blessed as part of our family heirlooms?"

Kennedy shook her head as a sly smile creeped across Caris's face. "Something changed and now you remember," Caris said.

"Yes. Whatever Mama saw and through her interaction with you in the past, spurred her into making changes to our history. In this instance," Trin held up the bowl, "she purposely broke our scrying bowl then repaired it with a spell. She told me once that this was just one of the tools that would help us with our future endeavors, so I know there has to be others," Trin explained.

"What about her necklace you have?" Jason asked.

"Yes. You're right, I'm sure it served as one of the tools, but I've already used its magic when we battled Heinrich, so I don't think it could help us now," Trin explained.

"But in this time, it should still have its magic held within, yes?" Kennedy asked.

"Yes, but think about it. If we used it now, then the magic we need for that battle in the future wouldn't exist. It would have already been spent here," Trin shrugged. "I know it's hard to keep our heads wrapped around things as they change, but trust me, I think Mama has left us with the tools to use at just the right moments that will help protect us and our future. Here and now...it's this scrying bowl, I'm sure of it. So let's eat our breakfast and get started on the spell. We can search for the other tools later once we stop Ann and return to our current time," Trin suggested.

The group nodded then settled down to eat, excited by Trin's obvious enthusiasm at finding another item their mama had left for them to use in their time of need.

After washing down their breakfast with the juice Nadie left for them, Trin and the girls immediately began to prepare for the scrying spell they'd be casting today. "Caris, I'll need you to go to the river and gather some water." Trin turned to Jason. "Please go with her. I don't want any of us venturing out alone at this point."

Jason nodded and kissed her cheek then followed Caris from the wigwam.

"Kennedy, I'll need you to gather anything you feel will be a good representation of Ann from our time."

"Jesus, like what? It's not like we have a piece of her clothing or a strand of hair lying around."

"Perhaps one of your dolls will suffice," Trin winked.

"Oh man...I haven't thought of those things in forever." Kennedy laughed. "How many do you think I made that summer?"

"Honestly, I lost track. I just knew it was your way of healing after Mama passed. You never used them with ill intent, only as a way to find solace within your grief, so I didn't mind." Trin continued. "You had one for each of us, including Jason, Papa, and Ms. Bishop, and also for a few of your friends from town. You were adorable."

The sisters' laughter filled the hut as they worked side-by-side to prepare the spell. Kennedy constructed the doll for her representation magic, while Trin pinched some of the lavender she'd picked from the woods into the bottom of the bowl. Caris and Jason returned from the creek and joined them on the center of the floor next to the low-burning fire just as they finished.

"Are we ready?" Caris asked.

"Almost." Trin squeezed her sister's hand in gentle thanks as she took the skin full of water from her grasp. "Kennedy, will you and Caris cast circle around us?"

"Of course."

Kennedy and Caris stood and moved to take their place on the opposite sides of the fire, each standing behind Trin and Jason who remained seated. Taking a deep, grounding breath, Caris began. "I cast this circle, once around, all within magic bound. Protected from harm, and shielded this day, let the Goddess's light show us the way." They walked deosil in unison as Caris's magic rose to produce the first layer of energy in their sacred space.

"I cast this circle, twice around, all within magic bound. Cleansed with water and strengthened with earth, safe from harm with Spirit's mirth," Kennedy added, sprinkling salt and water from the palm of her hand.

"We cast this circle, thrice around, all within magic bound. Inspired by air and sealed by rite, protected from harm by Spirit's might," they finished in unison, each blowing a glowing breath to seal their magic in place.

"Thank you." Trin nodded to each of them as they reclaimed their seats around the fire.

From the skin, Trin poured a steady stream of water over the lavender snips and the miniature doll, filling the scrying bowl until it was halfway full. Raising the vessel into the air, Trin released it and sent it floating into place above the flames. Instructing everyone to stand, she handed each of them a piece of black string. "Wrap one end around your index finger and hand the other end to the person next to you who will then tie it off to their thumb, connecting us to each other."

Trin led by example, demonstrating exactly what she needed them to do. After everyone's string was criss-crossed and tied off between their thumbs and fingers, a net had been formed, leaving only a circular opening in the threads right above the scrying bowl.

Trin inhaled a deep breath as the flames boiled the water and permeated the air with the scent of lavender and magic. "Focus your energy up and down the strings, exchanging and sharing our magic like we did in the woods," she guided the group.

Caris, Kennedy, and Jason did as Trin asked without thought. The magic being passed between them flowed freely and energized the strings, sparking them to life. Trin smiled as power sizzled along the threads. "We're ready. Now repeat after me. Goddess of love, Goddess of light, join us for this important rite. Guide our magic, straight and true, finding the one at odds with you." She nodded at Caris who repeated the spell, then Kennedy followed suit, with Jason finishing up after her. "Now all together," Trin instructed.

"Goddess of love, Goddess of light, join us for this important rite. Guide our magic, straight and true, finding the one at odds with you." They all chanted together, repeating the spell three more times.

A collective gasp escaped the group as the water froze solid. The fire continued to pop and snap, caressing the bowl with its warm fingers as a purple light radiated from the repaired crack in its side. Trin, Jason, and her sisters stood in place, so as not to disturb the strings still pulsing with golden magic between their fingers, but leaned forward to peer over the edge to see what was happening within the bowl. The lavender snips shifted rapidly beneath the surface, attaching themselves to the doll representing Ann that was illuminated by the glow. Suddenly, a surge of purple light shot up through the opening of their web, projecting an image onto the roof of their skin-covered hut.

Kennedy gasped. "Oh my god, it can't be!" There, clear as day, was an outline of Tawni, the young Indian maiden who had befriended Kennedy and led her to the portal trees in the first place.

"Stay still. We need to end the spell and close the circle." Trin's voice was stern but rang with a soothing calmness.

As the energy in the room died down, Trin brought the spell to a close. "My Lord and Lady, thank you for joining us to witness this sacred rite. Your magic and guidance have led us true, blessed be, and thanks to you."

"Blessed be and thanks to you," the group repeated, as the threads of their web dissolved and fell from their fingers and into the fire.

"Caris, can you close the circle, please?" Trin asked, still focused on the task at hand.

"Of course." Caris raised her right hand and pointed her index finger at the circle to pierce the energy surrounding them. "I part this circle, all is done, magic forged by moon and sun. To all who came here thanks to thee; go in peace and blessed be." The energy dissipated by sinking into the ground, leaving the hut charged and protected.

"Okay, so clearly we've been fooled again by Ann's shape-shifting ways," Kennedy snapped. "But how is that possible if she doesn't have her full power?"

"I'm not sure but assume it has something to do with her finding her siblings," Trin replied. "All I know is that we now have a leg up and we're not going to waste it." She walked over and retrieved one of the baskets Nadie left with their breakfast and handed it to Kennedy. "You're going to go help little *Tawni* gather more trinkets in the woods today, and we'll be there, lying in wait."

"Good morning, Tawni! I thought with the free-time we have today, maybe you'd like to return to the woods so we can gather more shells and nuts for your gifts." Kennedy's smile never wavered as she stood outside the impostor's hut.

"Oh, Mama, can I please go with Ketnu?" Tawni bounced on the balls of her feet as she waited for her mother's reply.

"Of course, just be back before dark."

Kennedy nodded then followed the bubbling, bouncing fraud down the path and into the woods.

"Thanks for coming to get me, I was going crazy at the thought of being cooped up inside all day." Tawni kicked a rock from the trail.

"Of course, I promised I'd help and today seems like as good of a day as any." Kennedy grinned, forcing her teeth to unclench.

"How are your sisters doing? And the new warrior that joined the tribe last night," Tawni asked.

"They're fine. Just focused on doing a good job to make sure we help the tribe in the best way we can."

"It's a blessing our tribe took you in. I've seen others who weren't so lucky." Tawni continued walking, straight-faced and revealing nothing of her true self.

"Really? Like who? I've only ever seen your tribe show kindness and acceptance to strangers."

"That's because Nadie spoke for you all. She's the Chief's daughter, you know."

"No. I hadn't realized that. But you're right, it was a blessing she spoke for us and we're so grateful that your tribe accepted us upon her word." Kennedy fell quiet, contemplating exactly how Ann could be pulling off this ruse.

If Tawni was a real member of the tribe, did that mean there was a little Indian girl somewhere, tied-up or dead, while Ann paraded around pretending to be her? Or was Ann's illusion just that, a figment meant to fool everyone into believing Tawni was a part of their tribe when in reality, the girl didn't even really exist?

"Tawni, the last time we were here, you said that the trees really speak to you. What did you mean by that?" Kennedy asked, hoping Ann would stumble and reveal the witch she was.

"Just what I said. I find peace within this forest and when I'm alone I can hear them speaking to me."

"What do they say?" Kennedy asked tentatively.

"That an evil is spreading across the land, and that I should be careful."

"What kind of evil?" Kennedy palmed the arrowhead knife Jason had made for her earlier this same morning.

"A woman and her sisters." Tawni turned and met Kennedy's wide eyes just as they approached the portal trees.

Chapter Twenty-Six

"Grab her!" Trin exclaimed as she jumped from behind a nearby bush.

Kennedy snatched Tawni by the arm, yanking her close and holding the makeshift knife to her side.

"Ketnu, what are you doing? I don't understand."

"Stop playing games, Ann. We know it's you," Caris spat as she joined her sisters from behind the trees.

"Ann?" The young girl frantically shook her head. "My name is Tawni, and I'm your friend. Why are you doing this to me?"

Trin frowned and approached cautiously, reaching out and placing her fingers against Tawni's temples. The young maiden calmed instantly as visions from her life filled Trin's mind—her excitement at meeting Kennedy and finally being able to talk to someone new, the sweet first kiss she'd shared with a particularly shy Indian boy, and the sorrow she shared with her family when they lost her oldest brother in the war.

Digging deeper, Trin focused her thoughts on Ann and tried to draw out any magical tie that lay within Tawni's memories. Caris, Kennedy, and Jason stood still while she worked, not wanting to disturb their psychic link.

"There," Trin whispered. "I see it." Trin pulled her hands away from the young girl's temples and held her gently by the shoulders. "Tawni, I'm sorry we scared you, but just like you, we too have felt an evil in this forest. Today, when we went searching for it, we were guided to you, but it's okay. I now understand why."

"Care to share?" Kennedy asked impatiently, as she stuffed the knife back into her waistband.

Trin turned to face her family, taking hold of Tawni's hand. "Because Tawni carries a very special magic within her. She *is* able to speak to the trees and that's why we were guided to her by our spell. Not because she *is* Ann, but because the trees told her where to find Ann, and more importantly...how to stop her."

Everyone looked at Tawni as she wiped her eyes and smiled. "The trees here do what I say, so just tell me how I can help."

Two hours later in the softening light of dusk, Trin, Caris, Kennedy, Jason, Nadie, and Tawni all crept towards the burrow where Ann and her sisters had been hiding. Shown to Tawni by the trees, the hidden grove had been buried after a battle in the surrounding forest earlier that same season.

"Are we all clear on the plan?" Jason asked.

Receiving affirmative nods and a couple of thumbs-up, Jason led the way to the opening and motioned for everyone to fan out. Standing in a semi-circle, blocking the entrance to the burrow, they readied themselves to face the enemy within.

Tightening her grip on her rustic weapon, Kennedy stepped forward. "Ann Putnam, come out and face us. It's time for you to go home."

A malicious laugh drifted from the hole in the ground, followed by a bank of sickly gray fog. "Home? What would you know of home? Your sister made sure none of us had that pleasure the moment she cast her selfish spell."

"That spell saved us of all, including you. Do you think Heinrich would have let you live after he'd feasted on the last witch alive? No! He would have turned on you just like he did in the cave," Caris snapped.

The fog parted and out stalked Ann dressed in all black. Her fingers were marred with an inky substance that matched the dark circles around her eyes. "DO NOT SPEAK HIS NAME!" she screamed, waving her arms wildly in the air.

The sky split with a thunderous crack and rain pelted down on the group in an angry deluge.

"Aww, still sore that your boyfriend left you high and dry?" Kennedy egged her on, exactly as planned.

"He is my past, but now I have a bright future. One in which none of you will exist."

"Oh yeah, about that..." Trin stepped forward, holding Tawni's hand. "Now," she whispered to the young maiden.

Tawni knelt down, digging her fingers into the ground to tap into the roots of the surrounding trees. Branches swayed overhead as a protective umbrella formed over the group, shielding them from Ann's pounding rain.

"What is this?" Ann cried out.

"This is the Goddess's magic, and your foul attempt at harnessing or changing things in her world have come to an end." Kennedy stepped forward, her knife raised in one hand and magic pulsing in the other. "You and your sisters will leave this place and stop attempting to alter the timeline, or we will destroy you here and now."

Roots shot out of the ground, circling and ensnaring Ann where she stood. Screams and yelps rang out from the burrow as Tawni's magic guided the trees up through the ground, stopping Ann's sisters inside before they could join the fray.

"The outcome of this battle is up to you, but you will stop fighting one way or another," Trin stated flatly. "Please make the right choice."

Ann struggled against the rough bark, scraping her skin and making it clear she wasn't quite ready to give up the fight just yet.

"How dare you!" she screamed.

"How dare us?" Trin stepped forward. "Seriously? The Goddess gave you a great gift when she blessed you with magic all those years ago, but from that moment on, you've done nothing but squander and taint it with your poor choices. You could have lived out your life with your family and a coven who cared for you, but instead, you've spent your entire existence immersed in a dark magic that has only led you to heartbreak and failure again and again. When will you learn, Ann?"

"When will I learn? Ha! When will you learn to stop meddling?" Ann's eyes rolled back into her head as she started to chant under her breath. "Great Father bring me back to thee, so that together we may end the three. Through time and space hear my cry, remove me from this witch's eye."

Tawni reacted first, slapping a root over Ann's mouth, but it was too late. There, just below Ann's feet, opened a dark portal, sizzling with magic and cracking of lightening.

Trin watched in horror as a figure reached through the opening and grabbed Ann by the ankle, burning away the roots holding her with a familiar red energy. The memory of the mangled chord that twisted between her, Ann, and the demon pulled at her chest.

Time fell away as Trin was pulled forward, one step, then another, until she was poised on the edge of the portal.

"No!" screamed Jason.

Trin looked down, ready to face Heinrich once again, but was shocked to find not only one, but two familiar faces instead.

"I did as you instructed, Papa, I altered my destination and you were right, we will emerge victorious this time around." Ann smiled and sunk through the portal into her father's waiting embrace while Trin stared, mortified, into the eyes of her very own mother.

"I'm sorry, Karina."

Her mama's whisper rang in her ears as the portal snapped shut at her feet.

Epilogue

"Trin!" Jason exclaimed as he ran to her side, gathering her in his arms. "What did you see?"

"It was Mama," she sobbed. "She was there with Ann's father." Trin's head shook in disbelief. "She said she was sorry."

Caris and Kennedy knelt beside her, while Nadie comforted Tawni, praising her for being so brave and strong.

"What do you mean, it was Mama?" Kennedy asked.

Tears quivered at the edge of Trin's eyes as she looked at her sisters. "I mean, the Putnams have our mother."

Caris sank to the ground and started to cry as Kennedy stomped into the burrow, returning as she shoved her knife back in place. "They're gone, clearly escaped through the same type of portal. The only thing left are seven burnt circles on the ground."

"I don't remember their father having powers," Jason stated. "Maybe it's just another alteration that Ann created by everything she's done here."

"It doesn't matter." Trin wiped her eyes and pushed to stand. "Whether he had powers originally or not, he does now, and that means only one thing."

Caris's breath hitched on a cry and Kennedy helped her to her feet, both knowing what was coming next.

"We have to go back. We have to go back to 1685 and save Mama, or all our futures will be lost." Trin reached for her sisters, hugging them tightly as the Goddess's voice drifted through the air.

"You are my chosen three, Sisters of Salem forever you'll be. Follow your heart, your path is true, trust in yourselves, for I believe in you."

The End

About the Author

Award Winning Author, Tish Thawer, writes paranormal romances for all ages. From her first paranormal cartoon, Isis, to the Twilight phenomenon, myth, magic, and superpowers have always held a special place in her heart.

Tish is known for her detailed world-building and magic-laced stories. Her work has been compared to Nora Roberts, Sam Cheever, and Charlaine Harris. She has received nominations for a RONE Award (Reward of Novel Excellence), and Author of the Year (Fantasy, Dystopian, Mystery), as well as nominations and wins for Best Cover, and Reader's Choice Award.

Tish has worked as a computer consultant, photographer, and graphic designer, and is a columnist for Gliterary Girl media and has bylines in RT Magazine and Literary Lunes Magazine. She resides in Colorado with her husband and three wonderful children and is represented by Gandolfo, Helin, and Fountain Literary Management.

You can find out more about Tish and her all titles by visiting: www.TishThawer.com and subscribing to her newsletter at www.tishthawer.com/subscribe

Still want more?
Turn the page for an excerpt from
HOLLI'S HELLFIRE,
Book 3 in The Women of Purgatory Trilogy.

Excerpt

by

Tish Thawer

According to Norse tradition, Hel is one of three children born to Loki and Angrboda. Her face is described as half in light and half in darkness. She is half dead and half alive. Her face is at once beautiful to look upon and at the same time, horrific in form.

1

"Garrett, I swear, we'll get her back." Raven knelt below her best friend's throne as he grieved for the woman he loved. Her heart sank as she looked into in his cold, dead eyes. "Michael and I are working with Abigail and Asmodeus to find a way into Hel. We'll figure it out, I promise."

Death blinked at Raven's mention of Hel. It was a place and a person, but only one held his heart in her hands.

Holli, aka the Goddess Hel, had become Garrett's wife when he'd assumed the role of Death and became the leader of Purgatory and all its Reapers. This, of course, was only after Loki—Hel's father, had tricked them all with his twisted plan to unleash her and the *previous* leader of Purgatory into the mortal world in hopes of plunging the realms into utter chaos—the bastard. Thankfully, Garrett—with the help of his best friend and head Reaper, Raven, and her heavenly consort, the archangel Michael—thwarted Loki's plan not once, but twice. However, this time, they had all paid a heavy price.

Garrett looked down, meeting Raven's gaze with his sad eyes. "Thank you. Please keep me informed if you find a way into Hel." Raising his scythe, he disappeared in a cloud of smoke and shadow, most likely returning to the alternate castle which he and Holli had shared.

"Oh my god, Michael, we have to do something! I've never seen him like this." Raven stood up and threw her hands in the air, flaring her massive black wings. "Isn't there anything Heaven can do?"

Michael didn't respond but simply held out his arms and welcomed her into his waiting embrace. Their wings brushed against one another's, his pure white to her stark black. "I've already asked and the answer is still no. Holli has blocked all access to Hel, and until we find a way around that, I'm afraid the only thing we can do is wait." He kissed the top of her head as he wound his fingers under the curtain of her long raven hair.

Icy fragments climbed up her legs as the portal behind her continued to drag her down. Raven's scream pierced her ears while her husband raced to reach her, struggling to pull her back out of the void. "Ahhhhh!" she cried out and closed her eyes as a sharp pain erupted along the left side of

her face.

She heard Abigail ask , "Oh my god! What's happening to her?" and wondered the same thing herself.

It was then that she understood.

Holli's eyes snapped open. Time stood still as she stared at them all through her now mismatched eyes. One was still the beautiful bright blue, while the other was a black speck inside a frozen empty socket.

"Holli, my love?" Death gasped.

"My name is Hel, now please, let me go." She yanked her hand from her husband's and disappeared into the frost.

Holli woke to the sound of her own screams—again. The memory of falling through the portal and back into Hel continued to replay over and over in her mind. Cradling her half-collapsed face in her hands, she wept tears of ice from the bedroom of her frozen castle.

After being pulled through Loki's portal, she'd arrived on the ice-covered steps of her previous home, fully aware of her role as the Goddess Hel. Images of the souls that needed to be judged began bombarding her instantly, but all she could do was cry at the loss of Garrett and her friends. In an effort to escape her old life and the duties that came with it, she'd raced through the front doors and into her throne room where she cast a protective spell to block out the magic of her realm. It was her hope to remain sealed inside until Garrett found a way to save her.

Made in United States
North Haven, CT
18 August 2023

40472076R00138